T0129025

Diary of an (Un)Glamourous Model

HAZEL LORRAINE

ISBN: 978-1-4669-1089-8 (sc)
ISBN: 978-1-4669-1088-1 (e)

Trafford rev. 01/27/2012

 www.trafford.com

North America & International
toll-free: 1 888 232 4444 (USA & Canada)
phone: 250 383 6864 ♦ fax: 812 355 4082

Contents

PART ONE

Chapter One	Happy New Year!	3
Chapter Two	The Day Job	9
Chapter Three	The Bosses	15
Chapter Four	Guess Whose Back?	19
Chapter Five	He Loves Me, I Love Him Not	23
Chapter Six	The BFF	29
Chapter Seven	Model Impression	35
Chapter Eight	The (Soon-To-Be) Man	41

PART TWO

Chapter Nine	Opportunity Knocks	47
Chapter Ten	The L.A Doctor	49
Chapter Eleven	Off to La-La Land!	53
Chapter Twelve	Going Back To Cali	55
Chapter Thirteen	Mr. Chow-Wow	57
Chapter Fourteen	Good Gig, Bad Ex	67
Chapter Fifteen	Photo Shoot from Hell	77
Chapter Sixteen	I hate V-Day	85
Chapter Seventeen	Good Bye Cali	93

PART THREE

Chapter Eighteen	Home, not, so sweet home	101
Chapter Nineteen	Oh, What a Night	107

Chapter Twenty   I Hate Hospitals..........................113
Chapter Twenty-One   Bad Day at work 119
Chapter Twenty-Two   Greasy Chinese Take-Out 123
Chapter Twenty-Three   Weekend Fun..............................127
Chapter Twenty-Four   An Interesting Proposal 135
Chapter Twenty-Five   Told You So!................................139
Chapter Twenty-Six   The Last Time.............................143
Chapter Twenty-Seven   It's Over.......................................147
Chapter Twenty-Eight   Not Really Friends....................153
Chapter Twenty-Nine   Surprise, Surprise! 157
Chapter Thirty   Too Much Work..........................159
Chapter Thirty-One   Twiggy and Lezah 161

PART FOUR

Chapter Thirty-Two   Canned!.......................................171
Chapter Thirty-Three   Who is Duke Silverston? 179
Chapter Thirty-Four   Long-distance Calls Sucks.........187
Chapter Thirty-Five   No Where to Go 193
Chapter Thirty-Six   Too Drunk To Care 195
Chapter Thirty-Seven   Last Night in Toronto................203

PART FIVE

Chapter Thirty-Eight   Going to New York.....................207
Chapter Thirty-Nine   The Big Apple 211
Chapter Forty   Life is Grand 213
Chapter Forty-One   Photoshoot at Milk Studios 217
Chapter Forty-Two   New York Nights.........................221
Chapter Forty-Three   The End is the Beginning..........225

Dedicated to love

Acknowledgements

To my whole family, thanks for always being there for me. Special thanks to my sister Jennifer for always making me laugh. Love you always.

To my muse Damir Lolic—thanks for your love and support.

To my dearest friends Anne Ajero and Hon Chong—thanks for all the love.

To my whole team: Trafford Publishing and photographer Heidi Mehl. Thanks for your contribution to this book.

To God: I know sometimes I can be impatient, but I know you're there watching over me. Thank you for all the blessings you have given to me.

Lastly, to my readers thank you so much for your support. I wrote the book in love, I hope you enjoy it.

Part One

Chapter One

Happy New Year!

January 1, 2006
Mood: Extremely hung over

ANOTHER YEAR HAS arrived. Hello 2006! That means I can start again. (First, I need a Tylenol to get rid of this throbbing headache; last night's party was such a big blur. The last thing I remember is this model named Gabrielle trying to coerce me to have a threesome with some Brazilian air-head. Oh God, I had no interest because I felt my screwdriver coming up my throat. I drunkenly stammered away while Neil held my hair back while I puked in his newly renovated bathroom toilet. Now I'm here, can't believe I'm writing this down. I'm a sick drunk.)

But isn't that the craziest thing about New Year's? You can totally fuck up your life from last year and then wake up on January 1st and look in the mirror and say "Happy New Year! I'm going to change my life starting today." We all know in life shit happens, and it doesn't take long before life blows up in your face and you end up feeling helpless. Then you just have to wait again for the upcoming New Year to do it all again. (That's if you don't die from an accidental drug over dose, a subway altercation, or devastating break up that leaves you broken hearted and severely depressed standing on the top of a high rise building contemplating thoughts of suicide).

First things first, I have to make some New Year's Resolutions. And not only should I write them down, but I *have* to make consistent efforts to follow them. That's the hardest part, sticking to the changes you need to make in your life. I am so non-committal, but hey it's worth the try.

First resolution: Do not fall in love with unemotionally, pig-headed, selfish, unattainable men. These men are BAD. There was Baron Nelson, my erratic crazy ex-boyfriend from York University, who irreversibly turned me off forever from dating black men. I'm done with the brothers for good. Nothing against them but I think Baron's better off with a hoochie-mama-turned-baby-mama who shakes her arse in Kanye West music videos. I tried my hand at a relationship with a black man and after the three year fiasco that emerged from it—all the lying, the bloody manipulation, the cheating; I am counting my lucky stars that I didn't end up knocked-up in a dead-end relationship with a horrible man and collecting monthly welfare cheques to feed this poor bastard.

I, Lezah Santos, will focus on bettering my life with work and finding myself through the joys of singlehood. The sooner I accept the reality that fairy tale endings don't come true, the sooner I can avoid the bitterness that will seep through my life when I'll be enjoying the bittersweet life of a spinster. Oh great, is this the demise that all modern women experience before they've reached 40?

I shouldn't worry because I'm only 27-years-old and I look forward to spending most of my life alone. (Well not actually, but it's better to "hope for the best and expect the worse," especially when it comes to finding the perfect soul mate).

But where do you meet these so-called soul mates? Sometimes I take the subway in Toronto; I ask myself Will I meet my soul mate riding the Red Rocket?

Have you ever taken the subway on a Saturday night? All the single men are off to the bars to try to get laid while they're heavily drenched with cheap knock-off Armani cologne. I can't fathom that some woman is going to have meaningless sex with one of these losers who bought their cologne off the newsagent's counter.

I think that the idea of finding your soul mate and falling helplessly in love is just a fairy tale that never comes true.I feel sorry for the hopeless romantics out there; I just don't believe that it will ever happen to me. But I can't be so bitter in my twenties; everyone says it's the best time in your life. Mom and Dad always talk about their twenties as if it were the best of times; they emigrated from the Philippines to Canada as singles and met in Toronto. They dated, they partied, they fought a lot, but they smoked and drank and went to the Bee Gees concert. Sometimes Dad serenaded Mom by playing the guitar.

They got married after five years and had me when they were both 28 and my sister Cheryl at 32. Suddenly, that's when they stopped talking about their glory days of sex, drugs, and rock n' roll. Perhaps married life didn't sit so well for my parents because until this day they keep telling me, "If you get married, it won't be like how you live now. You spend too much money on clothes and boozing, and you and your sister party way too much! Remember if you get married, your freedom will suffer." It's almost like they both warned me about the perils of domestication. I wasn't afraid of getting married; I was worried about finding Mr Right.

But no matter how hard I try to believe that being a 21st century single person is the greatest thing on earth, I still don't understand why being dateless on a Saturday night makes you feel like the biggest turd on the planet.

The other day I talked to my closest childhood friend Angela Apito about singlehood. She's what I like to call Miss Bitter Bachelorette. Angela is an active single woman who works a 9 to 5 job and lives at home with her Filipino parents. She drives a Volkswagen Jetta and helps her family with everything. She's pleasant company, I've known her all my life, but she's just bitter about being single. These are the women who get 'offended' when they see couples make out in public or think that giving a blow job on a first date is a cheap way to start dating a guy. They judge other women on how they get men, and they feel extremely bitter that there aren't any decent men left in the world. Then they self-proclaim themselves liberal feminists and try to denounce men in their life, but still enjoy the occasional booty call or one-night stand if the guy fits their standards.

This is what Angela said about being single. "The best thing about being single is that you get to do whatever you want when you want without someone breathing down your neck. You can sleep with whoever you choose, but you can expose yourself to unwanted STD's and contracting HIV and the ultimate risk—becoming an infertile loser. So not only can you *die* from being single, but you can miss the opportunity of ever conceiving a child, and, therefore, becoming a massive failure to lend a hand to procreation. Most single people suffer from a break up that might take years to get over and will, most likely, involve spending thousands of dollars on a shrink who will record your emotional fuck-ups and sexcapades in your own personal file folder that will sit neatly in a filing cabinet collecting dust well after you're gone." She says taking a deep drag off her Matinee cigarette.

Wow, if I spend any more time with another Miss Bitter Bachelorette, I'll end up creating a support group similar to Alcoholics Anonymous called The Bitter Bachelorette Club. "All bitter single women over 35 are invited. Complimentary tea and coffee—bitch your heart out!" Would be written in the email.

All these women just want love, sex, and a yearly anniversary gift. I don't think Miss Bitter Bachelorettes *want* to be bitter. They just need a strong man to treat them right. When Angela was in a long-term relationship with Ryan Horvath, her cunning Hungarian boyfriend, she was entirely a different person. She laughed a lot because she was getting laid regularly and she smoked less. But when he dumped her for someone younger (she's only 28, he's 29, and the younger chick is 25) she turned into Miss Bitter Bachelorette almost immediately, "I hate men! I don't get them, one day they want you, the next day they want someone else. What's there left? Lezah, I think I should just become a lesbian."

"Now if you did that, you'll just end up hating women as much as you hate men. You're not even a vegetarian; imagine eating fish, instead of meat for the rest of your life? One day I was dyking it out with a woman, I felt like after eating her out that I just had a bit of fish. I wanted more, I wanted meat. That's when I realized that I wasn't a dyke. I would miss being with a man."

"Lezah! You've been with a woman?" She said shocked.

"Yeah, two of them. Two different experiences, but I don't think I'm bi-sexual. I was just bi-curious. The first time was a sexual experiment while I was at York and the second time I blame it on a lot of alcohol and a sweet French model who I just couldn't resist. I just wanted to experience what it was like to be with another woman. It was on my 'Been There Done That' list of things I wanted to do in my life."

"What else you got on that list?" She laughed.

"I want to go skydiving and join the mile high club. And you?"

"I'd like to have sex with a guy that I'll eventually marry." She said.

"Every thing's going to be alright. The right man for you is out there you just haven't met him yet."

That's standard practice for me; I use that phrase with every woman I meet. I even have to remind myself every day that maybe, just *maybe*, I haven't reached that level of bitterness just yet.

Chapter Two

The Day Job

January 3, 2006
Mood: Still tired

I LIKE MY JOB for now—as jobs go. It's something different and I still get to meet so many kinds of people and, luckily, no one gets on my nerves. I work on "Barely a News Show" an internet and TV show that showcases nude newscasters. We pre-record our news clips in a studio based in Toronto and we disrobe out of our suits as we read the teleprompter. Some people hate it. Some people love it. Some people just don't care about it. It's a show that has nudity, but the funny thing about the job is that the cast spends 80% of the time fully clothed at the studio. We get a lot of amusing fan mails asking us if we all attend meetings—au natural. They assume it's a naturalist environment, but the harsh reality is it's a real job where the cast spends enormous time preparing for the show.

When we have to show up to our contractual meetings, viewings, and briefings we get dressed up in professional suits and designer cocktail dresses. For the cast parties, the ladies love to sport their newest pairs of Jimmy Choo shoes and sexy D&G cocktail dresses.

I got hooked up with this when I auditioned for the show when they were seeking new female newscasters in Toronto last year. Many aspiring model slash actresses auditioned for the three co-starring spots, and I got one of them. That was the deal that I signed on the dotted line.

I was fine with it at the time because all my auditions weren't going anywhere spectacular. The business was tough. I was working as a model, but I wanted to get into acting. After about thirty auditions, I landed a bit-part as a doctor in a medical documentary. My bubbly agent Grace McDonald said that my scene was going to be used in a training video for hospital employees. Just great.

By the age of 27, I had an impressive resume filled with cashier work starting at McDonalds, Dairy Queen and Super Foods. So I started out at the bottom just like everyone else. After four years of working in the food industry, I worked in retail as a bookseller for Samson Books. Then I got a summer job as an airport lounge waitress (I was terrible and quit just after two months). My experience ranges from working in an office as a data entry clerk and receptionist to teaching autistic children for a psychological institute. I also took up supply teaching on the side.

But with all that experience, I just caved in to the show because a) I needed the money to pay off my debts and b) nothing ground breaking was happening in my acting career.

After graduating with a Bachelor's degree in psychology at York, I've just been doing the photo shoots at the hair shows for Lou Lou Shampoo and Aveda. So that's pretty much all of the modelling gigs that I get.

I can't complain about landing this gig on a TV show. I had my reservations about going all nude, but as a model you don't know when your next gig is going to be. So that's why I decided to try it out.

I've also asked my beautiful younger sister Cheryl to stay with me in our two-bedroom flat located at Lakeshore in the west end of Toronto. So that we can split the costs of the rent, without having to eat bread and water all month long. But what bothers me the most about this job is that my parents aren't happy that I'm working on this show. I was very close to my parents before all this modeling happened, but now they just can't seem to accept that I'm working on the show. They feel ashamed and embarrassed about what I do, so we don't talk about it. Every week my Dad will ring me to see if we're doing well, and he only asks me one thing, "How's your job?"

"It's going fine."

"They pay you on time?"

"Yup."

"Good, so I hope you can afford to pay your bills."

Since I started working on this show, I feel like the estranged daughter who is a disgrace to the whole family. My Mom doesn't even mention it to me; she barely calls me to ask about my job. When she does call it's only to check up on us to see if we're cleaning up the flat and gargling this new non-alcoholic Listerine that she gave to us. And that's the end of that subject.

But working on the show is great. The other ladies are cool, we get on well. It's shocking that you can put so many strong-willed women in one place and they all become friends; we're not catty, so far! From what I've seen the cast and crew is friendly (and intensely wacky) because we love to have fun. Women can get on in a friendly way on a TV show because they give each other their distance. We all have our own personal agendas and reasons why we're doing the show, so we're close, but we don't get too personal.

But today as we came back to the show after a week-off from shooting, we uttered unenthusiastic New Year salutations to each other while quietly getting ready for our segments.

We weren't up to our usual up-beat chatter; it was like all of us were nursing a massive hangover. We were all partied out as it showed on our faces and utter lack of energy to get into character. I was still popping Tylenols while my co-star/ colleague Appleonia Timmons was popping uppers in the corner of our dressing room.

Usually, on a typical shooting day our dressing room is filled with eight to ten newscasters. We all talk about everything. There's like ten conversations going on at the same time. It's like a 'multi-conversation' in our dressing room.

The senior newscaster Valerie Stevens is usually putting on her make-up (she always shoots first because she is the star of the show) and the rest of us are chattering away while getting ready. We talk about the show from our opinions of casual sex to where to buy $20 jeans that will accentuate your butt. The married ladies exchange tidbits about what annoys them about their husbands, while the single ladies bitch about the losers we encounter in dating life.

I'm the observer at the job and get off on all the cast and crews unique personality quirks. Since I've started working on the show, I've become close friends with the Associate Producer Stacey Dean, a thirty-something-year-old married woman who proudly shows off her humungous Barbie Doll collection and enjoys extreme sports like the Edge Walk at the CN Tower. She was like our den mother around the studio and had a striking resemblance to Kirsten Dunst when she did up her eyes.

Stacey was the go-to lady on the set who could solve a scheduling problem to a broken nail. Sometimes when I'm not shooting, she invites me into her office to enjoy a cup of coffee.

One day I asked her what was better: married life or singlehood? She said, "Being single is better *sometimes*. Get married only when you're both ready because it's a strong commitment. When you're single you only got to take care of yourself. It depends. If you're okay with dying alone then maybe being single isn't that dreadful. But then who wants to get eaten by cats?"

Oh shit, it is true. Singlehood involves dying alone without anyone knowing that you've died. "Even married people can die alone, and get eaten by cats. Singlehood is fun to explore and see different people. It's also a time for sexual experimentation with things that you've only fantasized about. I've never been married, but I think marriage would be fun, especially, if you love each other. You can create your own world."

"Aw Lezah, you're very naive. I've been married for over seven years to Evan, and it's not that much fun anymore. He's a pain. Sometimes I wish I was single." She said gushing over a slight flashback of her singlehood days.

"What do you mean? You regret getting married?" I said shocked.

"Of course not. I love Evan dearly. It's just when you're single you can have meaningless sex with married people and sometimes those married people have crazy husbands who don't put the toilet seat down after they've taken a piss. Sometimes married people have to meet someone over the internet for casual affairs which consists of secret cocktail meetings at a bar across town so that you know your spouse won't ever catch you there. These married people are totally experiencing an adrenaline rush of having cheap sex in one of those motels that charge an hourly rate. Then it comes down to this moment when you're in the dirty motel bed you say to the guy 'fuck me, fuck me now!'" She screamed.

"Stacey! Did you take a little something, something before you came to work? You're acting weird. Are you having an affair?"

Suddenly, she sat back in her leather seat and regained her composure, "Lezah, you mustn't tell anyone about this! I don't know what got into me." She said sipping on a glass of water.

"Hey don't worry, I won't tell anyone that you're cheating on your husband."

"I'm not cheating on him; I'm just telling you how some married people *can* be when they're not sexually satisfied with their partner."

Wow, I took a sip of my coffee and thought that the other day it was Miss Bitter Bachelorette and now here we have Mrs Horny Rabbit. The one who is married wants to bang someone else other than her husband and the single one will probably bang the married man. Other than that, Stacey seems to love her husband. Evan works on the show with us as a full-time editor and they seem like the perfect couple. But after Stacey's little rant, I wonder if she is faithful to Evan?

Chapter Three

The Bosses

January 4, 2006
Mood: Blah

*O*N THE SHOW, Landers Tucson is my boss who I like to call Mr Dick. This morning I walked through the doors at 8:03 am and Mr Dick bellowed from his office, "Lezah, you're late!" I totally ignored him and made my way to the dressing room. We aren't cool with each other.

At first, we were friends. He started out as a newscaster on the male cast; he was just like one of us. But then five months ago everything changed when he turned to the 'dark side.' The moment he got his own office in post-production, he started bossing everyone around.

Don't get me wrong, he's a talented guy. Absolutely no one on the cast knows this, but Landers tried kissing me at the season premiere party at the Ultra Supper Club. But I just wasn't into him. After he was visibly drunk, he pulled me aside before I left the club and asked me if I had a boyfriend.

"Yes, I'm with someone at the moment." I said lying through my bloody teeth. I was single, but would never dare consider dating him.

"Well, that's a shame. I think we would make a great couple." He said putting his arm around me.

"Your breath reeks with alcohol." I said pulling away. Suddenly he went for it; the guy tried kissing me at the exit of the club.

"Landers, you're so drunk right now. I have to go." I said distracted.

"Just think about it. You and me can make some magic. Night!" He said all cocky. I shuddered at the thought of kissing him.

The next morning at the studio, we were all hung over from the massive drinking and drugging we all did at Ultra. We should've had the morning off because we were all sitting around feeling dirty and partied out.

When I saw Landers he never brought it up and I acted as if nothing happened at the club.

Then five months later he got the personal office and a promotion by executive producer Douglas Williams, who I like to call Mr Grumpy. Douglas is a sixty-something-year-old unhappily married affluent lawyer with one son and a big mansion in Forest Hill who is obsessed with copywriting his name on pretty much everything that he can get his hands on. One day during a meeting he was wiping his hands with a napkin and said, "I'm going to copy write my name on this napkin, and that'll mean that I'll legally own all of these napkin!" My God, what more can rich people think of to buy?

Douglas is a top notch lawyer who sits at his desk with file folders stacked so high that you can barely see him below the rim of his silver-framed bifocals.

He's usually polite and all the time frugal. He's nice when you talk to him about the weather and his family, but he becomes cold and detached when you mention the words money or salary increase in the conversation. He sometimes comes to the studio to hold meetings with us, but he usually works at his private practice.

So to keep the show on schedule he promoted Landers to be the on-site producer. Gradually, Landers started acting superior over us. The once 'prankster' co-star who we all used to clown around with, suddenly became the guy we all feared the moment he stepped into our dressing room.

To be honest, I'm not feeling so optimistic about this show. Because of this stupid failed kiss situation, my boss is out to terrorize me for rejecting his advances. I thought it was going to be a stepping stone to other TV gigs, but it's been just the same old stuff over and over again. Nude telecasts with me reading the teleprompter and doing some weather bunny spins. I'm in by 8 o'clock and out by 2 o'clock on good days. Sometimes I'm out by 5 o'clock if we are shooting for the TV edition aired on the Australian Comedy Network. Apparently, we're a big hit in the land down under.

So that's work it's extremely fun, and I have a lot of free time to work on myself and just chill and work on my craft.

As a model, I don't do anything unusual when I'm off. I look at it as work.

So when I'm chilling I just like to listen to the music of Prince and Mariah Carey. But I love all kinds of music from classic rock to hip hop. I get my inspiration from listening to music, looking at art, attending live concerts, and watching films. I'm an artist by heart.

The only thing that bothers me about the producers is they obsessively warn us about our appearance. One morning I had an Egg McMuffin at the studio for breakfast right before shooting at 8 a.m. I ate it, shot my segment and after Landers gave me a little pep talk about eating junk food and insinuated that I was going to get fat.

"So shoot me that I went through the McDonald's drive thru for a breakfast sandwich." I scoffed.

"I'm just saying that our cast members should pay attention to what they eat. Think about it, if you eat those every day you'll turn into a fat pig and *that* means you won't be on the show anymore." He snickered.

I rolled my eyes and sighed as I walked away, he annoys the hell out of me. So since then I have *never* brought any fast food into the studio, and I go to the gym three to four times a week and practice yoga weekly. This is so I can stay in shape. The yoga is just for quieting my mind and looking for inner peace when I'm utterly pissed off at my boss. But I do worry about the way I look and if I gain weight, I'm like any normal woman in the world who feels insecure about their body. So since then, I don't eat Egg McMuffins because I am afraid I'll turn into a fat slob.

But this Landers guy, I know I would *never* sleep with him, he's not my type. He's just a bit taller than me, and, come on; I'm only 5'2! I like men who are much taller than him, so that's where he lost most of his points. And quite honestly, his deep set eyes and black wavy hair slicked back with sticky gel doesn't ever turn me on one bit. I usually like men who are tall, have nice eyes, a friendly smile, and it's a bonus if he's got a killer body to boot.

Those are the bosses who pay me for the job where I can afford a comfortable life. A lot of my free time is devoted to my colourful friends whose private lives are filled with funny relationships, dramatic theatre, and a lot of all-night partying. Then there are the men who I encounter in the world that makes my life strangely fascinating, until this day I don't know why my life is such a freak show.

Chapter Four

Guess Whose Back?

January 5, 2006
Mood: Stressed

*W*HO LOVES SLEEPING in on the weekends? I do! I usually sleep in on the weekends and cherish the moments when I can get up any time I want. But on this cold Saturday morning, I was awakened by the phone call that any woman would dread. As I looked at the caller ID, guess who it was? It was the evil ex-boyfriend Baron Nelson. OMG, I just shuddered. I hesitated whether to pick up the phone, what does he want?

I haven't spoken to Baron in ages. I officially broke up with him two years ago after our catastrophic off-and-on relationship. I hate off-and-on relationships because they fuck with your moods. It's like an off-and-on relationship can turn you into a bi-polar person. One minute you're up, the next minute you're down. The next minute you're arguing about stupid shit, and then the next minute you're having amazing make-up sex. Too many extreme highs and lows. It's not healthy.

After three years of countless trips to a licensed shrink and reading self-help books like "Stop Dating Jerks" by

Dr. Joseph Nowinski; I even trained my mind during yoga sessions to prepare myself to walk away, once and for all, from my tempestuous relationship with Baron.

When I told him that we were done, he laughed and said, "We break up almost three times a month, what makes you think that this time it's for real?"

"I'm just done with you. When I try to feel love for you, I don't feel anything. I'm not even mad anymore. I'm just fed up with this bloody relationship. It's not going anywhere! I am out, starting now! That's why it's for real. Don't ever call me, text me, email me, message me, you got it? I don't ever want to see you again. Peace out." I said with confidence.

As usual, he got angry and told me that I was talking gibberish. So I left him standing in front of his house while he hollered, "Lezah, we're not done. Why are you over reacting again? The drama queen you are! Come back here!" He demanded.

I didn't even want to rebuttal as I slammed my car door shut and drove off into the night. That was the last time I saw him.

After I broke up with him two years ago, I just wanted to be alone and party until I was flat-out drunk.

Now here we were, two years later, and *he's* calling me. Wonder what this is about? I figured that this was one of those 'ex-boyfriend-courtesy-calls' when your crazy ex rings you 'out-of-the-blue' because you just, miraculously, popped into his mind. We all know that we're all guilty for calling our exes a year later to see if the sound of our voices will get them horny enough to meet up with us for cocktails and, possibly, a reuniting romp in the sack. It's the backslide.

"Hello." I said in my raspy 'I-just-woke-up' voice.

"Hello Lezah. Happy New Year!" I knew it; i was *just* a courtesy call.

"Happy New Year, Baron." I said nonchalantly.

"So how are ya? It's been awhile since we last talked."

No, really? I dumped your ass TWO YEARS AGO and told you never to call me again, I thought. "Yeah, for sure it's been a while. How's life?"

"Ah, you know same old, same old. I'm back from Montreal, finished up the season."

I tried not to sound so enthusiastic, "Great. So . . ." There was an awkward silence that made me yawn loudly.

"Did you just wake up?"

"Yeah, it's Saturday morning." Duh, what the hell does he want?

"Oh yeah, I remember you love to sleep in on the weekends." He said reminiscently.

"Baron, I'm not trying to be rude, but I told you never to call me again."

"Whoa, slow down there cowgirl, no need to get defensive. It's been over two years; I didn't think that you meant not to call you for the rest of your life."

"Well, you thought wrong. I *did* mean it when I told you to never to call me again. I have to go." I said about to end the call.

"Lezah, don't hang up. I just wanted to call you to say what's up. Can we talk? I mean, can we meet up for a coffee? I *have* to talk to you."

Since when did Baron have to talk to me? All we ever did was have sex, argue, and have make-up sex after we argued. I honestly wouldn't constitute that as *talking*.

"What do you want to talk about?" I said.

"Um, well, can't get into it over the phone. No pressure, but it's just that it's been so long . . . and I just got back into town."

I started getting irritated. Did he think that just because he was back in town, that he could just walk back into my life? I have grown so much from this stupid waste of a relationship that I wasn't about to be sucked back into relationship hell.

I sighed, "I don't think so. I'm pretty busy these days. If you have something to talk about, just tell me now."

There was silence. I felt nothing; I didn't want to see him at all. Before our break up, he would call me, and I'd feel butterflies in my stomach. Now the only thing I felt was the morning growl in my gut telling me that it was time to eat breakfast.

"Can't we just meet at the cafe by your place this afternoon, please? It won't take long."

Oh great! Never been here before, obsessed evil ex-boyfriend insisting to see me. How bad can it be? I already know that I don't love him anymore, so why do I keep agreeing to see him?

"What time?"

"Let's say around two o'clock."

"Just coffee?"

"Yup, just coffee." He promised.

"Okay, fine, but I don't have a lot of time. I have plans with my sister today." I had to lie. I didn't have any plans with Cheryl.

I hung up and lay in my bed thinking for a minute. To think that after two years of no contact, it took less than two minutes to convince me to meet my dreadful ex-boyfriend. And what's worse, what the hell did he want to talk to me about after all these years? I got so flustered that I put the covers over my head and screamed.

Chapter Five

He Loves Me, I Love Him Not

January 6, 2006
Mood: Liberated

*S*O I SHOWED up at Zing cafe looking F-A-B-U-L-O-U-S in a winter white Marciano dress that I was saving for a special occasion. At first, I was thinking that he didn't deserve to see me in such outfit, but then again, I had to rub it in his face what he *is* missing and *can't* have anymore.

Surprisingly, I wasn't nervous when he approached me in front of the cafe. He kissed me on the cheek while I casually patted him on the back. This was the new me, cool and detached.

When we sat down, I almost chocked. I can't believe that I stressed myself out so much for *this* guy; he looked like a five year old boy trapped inside a six foot three, over built, black football player who was probably on steroids. In those first three minutes of laying my eyes on him, I realized that I was over him. Thank God.

He barely aged, he was only 26. But he did get bigger from the last time saw him. I always had my suspicions that he was on steroids because at 6'2, he got so big, so quickly and weighed 250 pounds. He denied ever taking steroids, but one time I blamed his supposed steroid use on his explosive temper tantrums that would result in swearing tirades, and he still denied it.

At the cafe, he was wearing a black Adidas sweat suit while I caught a whiff of his heavily drenched Cool Water cologne that made me slightly dizzy. Definitely was *never* going to sleep with him again. He can totally forget it.

I regretted wasting a lot of my energy trying to make this so called "open relationship" work; he was and still is a pretentious chump.

"Wow! Lezah, you sure look good." He ogled.

Too bad I couldn't say the same for him. "And you look . . ." at that moment, I was at a loss for words, "the same."

It felt terribly awkward; Baron and I never met for coffee. In the beginning of our relationship he wined and dined me a few times (To come to think of it, *I* paid for our first date. He had the audacity to pull the "oh-I—forgot-my-wallet-at-home" act when the bill arrived and he promised that he would pick up the tab for our second date. Which *he* did, but that doesn't erase the fact that he was still a cheating, manipulative, unreliable boyfriend.)

Over a cafe latte, he told me that he wasn't going back to Montreal in the spring. When I asked him if he got traded to another football team, he shook his head in shame, "Lezah, I got released from the Alouettes at the end of the season."

My feelings were mixed. My initial reaction was to apologize for his release, but in the back of my mind, I was screaming "I told you so!"

This was the day I was waiting for—the day he would come back to me and return to being the same old Baron that I had met in the freshman year at York.

He still seemed a bit shocked, but I kept my poker face on and offered my sympathy, "Don't worry about it. I am sure you'll be able to get picked up by another team."

"No Lezah you don't understand. The league released me *altogether*. I am no longer eligible to play on *any* CFL teams." He said.

"Oh, so sorry to hear that. So what does this mean for you?"

"It means I am an average man now." He said.

I tried hard to keep my composure, but it was hard for me to pity him. But I could tell that his rather "larger-than-life" ego was severely bruised, and I started feeling this perverse pleasure from seeing him in dire straits, "I'm sorry Baron, I know how hard you worked to get into the league."

He took a deep breath, "Yeah, I know. But I guess I had it coming, all these younger players are getting recruited each year and I was injured in the past season. They just didn't have room for me on the team."

I nodded, "I understand. So what's next for you?"

He shrugged, "I don't know, just take it one day at a time. I think I'll get a job real soon, I have a few things lined up."

I tried to be supportive and rested my hand on his forearm, "You're a smart guy, and I *know* you'll find a job."

There was a brief silence between us and I knew something else was coming, "Lezah, I want to ask you something important."

Oh great, here it was, the real reason why he needed to talk to me, "Sure, what is it?"

"Are you seeing anyone?" He asked curiously.

"No one special, but I am dating from time to time." I had to slide that in.

"What do you think about giving our relationship another shot?"

OMG! I couldn't believe that he was asking me this. He's got a lot of nerve to call me up after two long ass years asking me for another shot.

Now that *he* has the time to start a relationship, did he think that he can just walk back into my life and get me back in a snap of a finger? No way! I put up with so much crap from him and now that he's feeling all lonely and vulnerable, he thinks that he can just call me up, invite me out to a ten dollar lunch and put through me through relationship hell again? What do I look like a martyr?

"Baron, I just can't do this anymore. I told you when we broke up two years ago that I was done, I meant it. *You* wanted the freedom to see who ever you wanted, so I let you go. I'm different now; I want to be in a committed relationship."

"That's why I called you because I'm ready to commit. I still love you." He said.

Say what? Did he just say that he loved me? I suddenly felt so sick to my stomach; Baron was still a manipulative man who thought that all he needed to do was throw out some cheesy love lines he heard from Usher and I would take him back. Well, he was in for a rude awakening. I wasn't buying it and I loved him—NOT!

I completely dismissed the 'I Love You' comment, "You just can't snap your fingers and say 'I'm ready to make a commitment.' My life has changed, I don't want a boyfriend right now. I feel happy that I'm single." God, I was so relieved to say that and mean it. Girl Power!

"So I'm guessing that's a no?" He asked with a hopeful look in his eyes.

"Of course it's a no. I don't want to get into anything serious right now and I know that we cannot get back together. We can be friendly, but that's about it." I said officially.

He looked so disappointed, even defeated. But that's how I felt for years. Not meant to be bitchy, but he deserved it. When we dated in university, he put me through relationship hell. He was the type that he would cancel and give me some lame excuse a few hours before our date. Sometimes I felt like an idiot because I had picked out an outfit that I was going to wear. Imagine how I felt when he cancelled while my whole outfit was laid out? I felt so humiliated. I wanted to burn those outfits; I even returned a dress once because I was so mad at myself for thinking that he would be there for me.

As years went by, it just got worse. He stopped calling me to cancel; instead, he would just turn off his cell phone. I would obsessively leave messages on his voicemail, but he never called me back. My friends warned me all the time that he was just using me, but I didn't want to believe it, I *always* made up excuses for him. I was a naive young lady.

"Lezah, you okay?" He asked. I snapped out of my gaze and saw before me my desperate loser ex boyfriend begging me for another chance at love. But where was *he* when I needed the love and support? He was probably at some other chick's house banging her brains out. But I wasn't going to let the past get into the way of the present.

"Yes, I'm fine. So is this what you wanted to talk to me about?"

"I want to get back together."

I shook my head, "Look, I just can't get back with you anymore. I've moved on and I'm happy being . . ."

He put out his hand motioning to stop, "Single. I get it, you're happy being single. I understand."

And that was that. This was a softer side of Baron, which I had never seen before. But then again he probably was down about life because his dream of becoming a star football player was crushed. Ha! I feel wicked for laughing at him, but then again good things happen to good people. And bad things happen to bad people. In this case, the bad boy's dream is over!

Chapter Six

The BFF

January 8, 2006
Mood: Content

*J*UST GOT OFF the phone with Neil and tonight there's going to be another exciting party at Pussy Palace. First let me explain.

Meet my crazy friend Neil Green. He is one of Toronto's successful modeling agents. He is the CEO of Metropolis modeling agency and has a roster of top models that walk the runways in London and New York and gain fame through international fashion magazines from "GQ" to "Elle."

Trust me, you don't want to mess with my gay BFF as he's a self-made man who is a retired model himself and is popular for being an outspoken divo. What's fascinating about Neil is that he has a striking resemblance to former "Vogue" magazine editor-at-large fashion icon Andre Leon Talley; the only difference is that he's darker than Talley. He's stocky, black, and has the swagger of a foul-mouthed thug. He looks like a tough guy from the outside, but once he starts talking, he's like Mariah Carey on crack. When he's dissatisfied with something like bad restaurant service he snaps his fingers in the air while he switches his neck from side-to-side. His favourite phrase is, "Oh no, you didn't!" Two snaps in a circle.

Neil is an attention seeker who loves his designer labels (he has no choice as he gets most of his clothes from his big-time clients like Calvin Klein and Hugo Boss). He's really nice when you meet him, but he can get catty with you because he is flaming gay.

What's so intriguing about Neil is that he's so passionate about his models. During his spare time, he's always on the lookout for fresh faces. He usually scouts the shopping centres and night clubs in other parts of Ontario looking for his next protégé. Neil's the kind of agent that will go all out for a model that he thinks has what it takes to make it all the way to the top of the modeling biz (and, of course, earn him a shit load of money).

Since a lot of these models are out-of-towners, most of them can't afford to rent an apartment in the city. So Neil has this three bedroom apartment which he calls his Pussy Palace sanctuary where his protégés can live in at the beginning of their careers. That's where all the models congregate. Every month, Neil throw's a party at Pussy Palace so that his friends (like me) can meet and party with his young family of giraffes. It's also a chance for him to play his wicked game of getting his male models totally wasted and then trying to coerce them to have sex. It usually ends up with him publicly apologizing to the whole party blaming his addiction to sex and alcohol as the main culprit for his perverse behaviour.

But Neil does compensate for his actions. He takes these amateur models under his wing; grooms them and then his photographer Sidney Jackson develops their portfolio books. Within a few weeks, he sends them off to various go-sees per day and once they start making money from their modelling assignments, Neil deducts portions of their rent from their first pay cheques.

Once they're established in the biz, they usually move out from Pussy Palace and get their own flats. Most models stay up to six months, then they move out, but once someone leaves, Neil recruits a new model to fill their spot. So there is always 'fresh meat' running around Pussy Palace, as Neil puts it.

The only catch with Neil is that you have to sign an exclusive contract with his agency and fork over the 20% commission for his bookings.

But other than that, Neil appears to be the quintessential model agent—he is relentless. He will not stop investing all his time and resources in launching his models.

But this darker side of Neil sometimes gets out of hand. As a horny gay man who likes to transform small town boys into top male models, he experiences these massive power trips when he starts to feel possessive over his models, particularly, the men. He thinks that most people are bi-sexual anyway and in some sick-and-twisted ideology he thinks that these male models owe him something. In this case, it's their buttholes.

Sometimes he's successful in bedding them, and most of the time he has to cry and beg for their forgiveness. There were a few of them that never came back to Pussy Palace and left the modeling biz once and for all. Neil convinces himself that he has never done anything wrong to these models. He loves and cherishes each and every one of them (even if some guys have run away covering their asses).

Almost a year ago, he met a very handsome man who waxed his Lexus at some local car wash in Windsor, Ontario. Neil was on one of his sporadic treasure hunts for fresh faces and once he got a closer look at the wax man, Neil knew *he* would be his next protégé.

He slipped him his business card and asked him, "Have you ever thought about modeling?"

Anthony Stevens tossed the business card in the trash can next to some pails and said, "Nope, modeling's for pussies."

Neil got out of his car and Anthony put his fists up. Neil flapped his hands in the air like the true fairy that he is and said, "No, no! I'm not going to hurt you. I just want to talk to you. I think you have a great look and I want to help you out. My name's Neil Green. I own Metropolis modeling agency down in Toronto." He said extending his hand out. Initially, Anthony was reluctant to shake it as he had never met a black man before from the capitol. But after their awkward introduction they had a friendly chat while Anthony waxed the next car.

Neil asked, "So what do you here for fun?"

"Just drink. You know, hit the bar, watch TV, help my folks out on their farm, and bang broads who are open to having a good time. No commitments, I'm not into relationships." He said wiping down the car in several sweeping motions.

"Are you happy at this job?" Neil said lighting a cigarette.

"This . . ." he motioned to the car.

"Yeah." Neil said taking a drag.

"A job's a job. I ain't got any complaints, but a man's gotta do what A man's gotta do. You know what I'm saying?"

"You didn't answer my question. Are *you* happy at this job?"

Anthony tossed the rag into one of the buckets sitting on the ground and the driver paid him $10, "Not really. Been doing this job for over six months now and the only thing that makes me smile is when I get paid."

"What if I told you that you could make thousands of dollars in a day's work and have your own place to live in and travel all around the world, would you take that job?"

Anthony thought about it for a moment, "Hey mister I don't know what sting operation you're running in Toronto, but over here in this town we locals don't believe in turning tricks to earn our keep."

"You won't be turning tricks to earn this money. You would be walking down a runway in Milan, Italy wearing designer clothes from Ralph Lauren and Gucci and your face would be plastered in every fashion magazine sold on the newsstands."

Anthony snickered, "Yeah right and now you're going to tell me that I just won a million bucks from the Publishers Clearing House."

"I'm serious. I think you have a great look that will take you to the top of the modeling business. Have you ever wanted to travel? Meet tons of people and sleep with the hottest women in the world?"

"Seriously, you sound like you're selling a fake holiday that we all know never happens to people like me."

"It could happen if you just gave me a chance." He said sincerely.

Neil locked eyes with Anthony showing him that he was indeed extremely serious about the offer, "Look, I don't know about all that modelling bullocks. I am just an average man who lives with his parents on a farm."

"But you could change that if you just come with me to Toronto for a day. I've got a fabulous photographer who will take some test shots of you. We'll send some test shots to some of my clients and see if you got a shot."

Anthony swung a clean rag over his shoulder as another car pulled up to the waxing station, "You say your name's Neil?"

"Yes, it's Neil Green. So what do you say?"

"Can you give me your card again?"

Neil quickly pulled out his silver plated card holder and handed him another one of his business cards, "Here you go.

Hold on tight to it and give me a call whenever you're ready. Trust me, you don't want to let go of this opportunity. I can make you into a big star."

Anthony looked at the card and this time he didn't throw it away, he slipped it into his pocket.

*   *   *

The following week Anthony quit his job at the car wash, rang up Neil, and drove to Toronto in his old Ford pickup truck and started living at the Pussy Palace.

After sending his test shots to some of Neil's valued clients, Anthony was immediately booked on different photo spreads and he shot up the male modelling world in a matter of months. He went to New York Fashion Week and walked on the runways of Dolce and Gabbana and the late Alexander McQueen.

It seemed like overnight that Anthony went from being a simple farm boy working at a car wash to one of the most sought out male models in the whole world.

In his first three months of modelling, he earned over $50,000 from runway shows and magazine spreads and he was living in a trendy studio loft on King Street, strategically, a few blocks away from Neil's agency.

Anthony adjusted quickly to living in the fast lane—he had it all. At the age of 25, Anthony had a top paying job as a male model, international travel under his belt, and his own flat.

After London Fashion Week, he came home and purchased a sweet Range Rover (but he still kept his old pickup truck for keepsakes). He was the 'It' boy of the city, and that's when I met him.

Chapter Seven

Model Impression

Date: January 10, 2006
Mood: Content

I MET ANTHONY STEWART briefly at a Toronto Fashion Week after-party held at the swanky Royal York hotel. Neil briefly introduced me to him while he was being swarmed by a pack of giraffe models who wanted to get him to the bar for some shots. When I met him in that split second, I was impressed. For once I understood what Neil saw in him that day he was at the car wash. He was 6 feet tall, had short dirty blonde hair, these bright blue eyes that graced his Botticelli face along with a killer smile. He was very masculine with a child-like innocence.

When we met he kissed me on both cheeks but some buzzed cut African giraffe who looked like Amber Rose pulled him away. C'est la vie.

So we made our way through the party schmoozing with everyone, all while trying to get to the bar.

When we got our martinis he said, "Can you believe that Anthony is straight?"

"I do believe that he's straight. Nothing about him screams gay to me."

"How can anyone that good looking and that nice be completely straight?"

I chuckled, "Oh Neil, if you could have it your own way all the good looking nice guys would be gay and submerged on a deserted island where all of you could fuck each other until your dicks fell off."

He laughed, "I like how you know how my mind works."

"Well, it's not that hard to figure out what's going on in that pretty little head of yours." I said sipping on my drink while glancing around the party. "So what's the deal with your protégé?"

"Ah! He's single and very much available." Neil said fanning his hand over his face.

"Really? That's hard to believe. Not!"

"He's single but he's met a girl in New York, don't know if they're serious, but don't tell anyone. I swore to secrecy that I wouldn't say anything, but I want to hook you up with him."

I laughed, "Now I *know* you're talking bullocks. You know guys like that never go for a girl like me?"

"Oh, stop it. You're exactly his type—smart, beautiful, sexy. If you want him, consider it done."

"Don't sweat the small stuff." I said drinking the end of my martini.

While we walked out to the party, Neil was holding my hand because he was completely wasted, "I'm not happy when I'm sober, I'm a absolute wreck. Look at me; I'm an old, fat, gay black man. Nobody wants me. Not even the gays." He said in a huff.

"First of all, you're not fat, you're just extremely buff. Second, you're 35, that is not old! Those gay men don't know what they're missing because you are the most successful and sweetest gay man I've ever met. You just haven't found 'the one' because you're too busy chasing *straight* male models."

We ordered another round of martinis while laughing, "Oh Lezah, that's why I love you so much. You always know how to make me laugh."

"Hey guys what's so funny here?" Anthony said coming up to us from behind.

"Anthony, darling!" Neil said while he put his arm around him, "Where have you been?"

"Here and there. Got to pay my respects to everyone in the party." He said eyeing me.

"Now that's my man. Business comes first." Neil said proudly.

"Sorry, I don't mean to be rude, but we met earlier and I didn't catch your name." Anthony said turning his attention on me.

"I'm Lezah." I extended my hand out to him and instead of shaking it, he kissed it. That's three kisses. Impressive, he's quite the charmer already.

"I apologize for not getting it right the first time. I'm Anthony."

"Yes, I know who you are. Your agent *here* told me all about you." I said motioning to Neil standing next to me.

Neil put his arm around me, "Anthony, I'd like you to meet my Bella. If I wasn't gay, I would marry this girl; she's a real keeper. You know, she's a writer and model—a *real* intellectual." Neil boasted.

"Very cool." He said taking a sip from his drink while shooting me his million dollar smile of pearly whites.

Neil was now totally wasted; all the martinis and smoking had fried his brain cells which made him complacent, "Excuse me, I have to go get me some ass. Oh no, you didn't! Have fun you two!" He winked at me and patted Anthony on his shoulder.

Thank God, finally a moment alone with the super model! At first glance, you would think that a conversation with a male model would consist of air-headed topics related from what hair gel works well to how tired his feet were from walking up and down so many runways.

But I was surprised because we didn't talk about anything model-related. It was refreshing to talk to someone who wasn't so self-absorbed, "So what do you write about?"

"Ah, you know, a little bit of this and a little bit of that." I joked.

"I'm interested. I just finished reading 'American Psycho' from Bret Easton Ellis. Ever hear about it?"

"Sure, I know the movie with Christian Bale. Saw it, loved it. Tried reading the book, but, unfortunately, all the name dropping of designer labels got a bit tiresome after the thirtieth page." I said.

He was amused, "So I guess you don't write about psychotic yuppie murderers who dress in Burberry scarves, Tommy Hilfiger gloves, and an Alan Flusser suit, huh?"

"Not a chance. I write about dating and relationships. The whole shebang. How to get a man, how to get a woman, how to kiss, how to make sex romantic—you know, all that good stuff."

"That's cool. I bet you don't need any help with that, you're an expert."

"Not quite, that's the beauty of writing about it. I try to learn from other people's experiences and then get it down on paper. Of course, if I have my own experience I throw it in there, but, usually a lot of my ideas come from people I meet."

"Oh! Does that mean that I'll be a character in your next article?" He said putting his hands up screaming 'I surrender.'

"Hmmm, maybe I'll write about you, if you're interesting enough."

"Ooh!" He said shivering, "If *I'm* interesting enough? I think you and I put together can make a very interesting story, no?"

"We'll see about that. It depends how good you are." I said mischievously.

We grinned at each other when suddenly a look-alike of an anorexic Heidi Klum came up to Anthony and whispered something into his ear. I always felt like the odd one out at these model parties, I'm the 5'2 midget who was totally non-existent amongst all of these lanky giraffes.

After she giggled Anthony turned to me and said, "Excuse me for a minute."

And presto, he was gone. She took him away from me just like that. I looked around to see if anyone had witnessed what had happened, but nobody cared. I tried scanning the place for Neil, but he was long gone. He probably got that piece of ass he was looking for. And as usual, I was the intellectual short girl who stumbled out of the party alone, unusually tipsy, and feeling hopelessly restless.

Chapter Eight

The (Soon-To-Be) Man

January 13, 2006
Mood: Excited

*G*UESS WHO EMAILED me today? My soon-to-be-man Jared Martinus! Oh yes, how could I forget this hot Slovak guy I met when I was on assignment in Vegas back in January 2005.

Reading his morning email perked up the rest of my uninspiring day at work:

> Hi Lezah,
>
> Happy New Year! How's my beautiful? We met a year ago around this time, remember?
>
> We had a good time in Vegas, and I'll never forget it. You ever think about coming to Europe sometime this year? Or how about New York? Cross your fingers, I might be going there in the Spring.
>
> Missing your sweet smile and kissing you all over your sexy body.
>
> Xoxo,
Jared

Even though meeting Jared was probably one of the best things that ever happened to me in my life, I feel weird professing about the basis of my 'love' for him—which if you think about it was a four-day sex romp in The Venetian with a European guy who emailed me from time-to-time.

But now I know my next New Year's Resolution: I *must* visit Europe this year! I'm thinking in the summer time I should visit him in Bratislava, it's going to be awesome.

But in all honesty, I had never heard of Bratislava before meeting Jared. But if the guys over there are just as hot as he is, well then I'm moving there someday and so are the rest of my girlfriends. I don't think I've ever met anyone so polite and attractive anywhere in my neighbourhood.

He sparked up a conversation with me while I was waiting for Cheryl and her boyfriend Andrew to come meet me at the grand fountain in The Venetian. I was on a four day modelling assignment and since Andrew enjoys gambling from time-to-time, they decided to tag along with me.

He looked heavenly when he smiled at me, and his icy blue crystal eyes shone through a set of crow's feet around his eyes.

When he spoke about his plans for the evening, it was at that very moment that I realized that I was talking to a foreigner, "Can I ask where are you from?"

"I'm from Slovakia. Ever hear about it?"

Have I ever heard about it? Hmmm. Slovakia. Whenever I meet people while I'm travelling, I have this system where I try to locate the country in my head and if I still have no idea where it is, I think about all the news that I've read or heard about this country. In this case, I had a clear answer, "Yes, I have. You guys like to play hockey, right?"

"That is true." He said gleaming.

Bingo! I have scored a goal. Now he thinks that I am a well-travelled young woman who knows all about European geography, "That's something we have in common. You see, I'm from Toronto and I love hockey."

His eyes suddenly lit up, "You are Canadian? So what are you doing out here in Vegas?"

"I'm here working on a modelling assignment. My sister and her boyfriend are here, somewhere. So what are you plans for the evening?"

"Nothing special was just going to order room service. And you?"

"I'm going to have dinner at Tao. You're more than welcome to join us." I said. Oh great, did I just ask him out? It was like a slip of the tongue, I don't like asking out guys. Call me old-fashioned, but it just wasn't my style. But it was too late, I opened my big mouth and threw the question out there.

"That would be great. I'd like to check out Tao, haven't been there yet." He said smiling.

Oh, damn that smile of his, it made me feel warm so inside. Dinner at Tao led to a night cap at Oculus and I had learned that Jared was a 30-year old videographer and editor for a production studio in Europe. We talked about everything from politics, entertainment, travelling, and relationships.

By the second day, we were hooked on each other. I slept with him that night after a romantic dinner at Sushisamba and a gondola ride through the Grand Canal. After that night, I realized that romance, sex, and lust do mix well together when you've got great chemistry. And that was the beginning of what I like to think of as 'My Vegas Fling.'

Part Two

Chapter Nine

Opportunity Knocks

January 28, 2006
Mood: Excited

GREAT NEWS! GRACE just rang me up and said that I'm going to L.A next week for a spokes modelling gig! Sweet! But I know Landers is going to have some comments for taking the week off to go to L.A. But that's how it is in the biz, when opportunity knocks; you got to learn to open the door. The show is built around promoting ourselves as personalities, but sometimes they get all defensive when you need to take time off from the show to do your own thing. But I keep reminding myself that my contract doesn't say anything about exclusivity, so I'm pretty much a free agent when it comes to landing other gigs.

Then there's Mr Dick who makes everyone feel guilty when we do something unrelated to the show that will help us out with our careers. He calls it "digressing from the show," but I call it jealousy. I think he's just jealous that he's stuck in the studio all day long and can't pursue outside interests like us.

Anyway, I told Grace to book it and that I was game. As usual like in Vegas, the trip is all expense paid—the airfare, the hotel and meals are all covered. They're also allowing me to bring a chaperone. I'm thinking about who I can bring that can get the time off from work. I can't bring Cheryl; she's working and in college and Angela works like a dog without any days off.

I know! I'll take my friend Raleigh. She's a laid-back model who does virtually nothing when she's not working. So hopefully she won't be booked and she can come to L.A with me.

Chapter Ten

The L.A Doctor

Date: February 7, 2006
Mood: Content

I JUST REMEMBERED WHO I can call in L.A—my friend Dr. Elgin Garner. He's a family friend of my cousin Teresa Santos in Glendale, California. I met him nearly six years ago while I was a guest at her traditional lavish Filipino wedding.

Elgin is a thirty-something doctor who has jet black hair and these intense brown eyes. He looks like a Hawaiian Keanu Reeves. He's attractive and very intelligent and dresses very stylish with Hugo Boss and Burberry as part of his wardrobe.

When I met him at Teresa's wedding I got the impression that he was more of the conservative type. When my cousin saw me talking to him at the wedding party, she pulled me aside and said, "He's a real catch, that one you're talking to. You do know he's in his last year of residency at the hospital? He's really sweet and goes to church regularly. I think it's great you both connected at my wedding." She beamed.

He was religious part of the Seventh Day Adventist—something you don't find in a lot in men nowadays. I haven't seen him since my cousins' wedding, but since we had such a good connection, we've kept in touch via email. My mother loves the fact that I met a doctor from California; she keeps insisting that I give him a chance. But there is something more than meets the eye. He's a good looking and successful doctor, but he was definitely reserved.

At the wedding he told me that he was doing his last year of residency but now six years later he is a licensed doctor—a paediatrician to be exact. He is very friendly and from what I know he is still single. Oh man, this is going to be exciting. It will be great to see him again.

*   *   *

This week was crazy busy at the studio. Valerie Claremont and a few other senior newscasters were chosen to be interviewed by an evening talk show called "Look Who it is." I wasn't chosen to be interviewed because their angle was focusing on women who were middle-aged and balancing a marriage while working at this non-conventional job. That totally ruled me out and I was kind of glad that I didn't have talk about my experience working on the show. I still don't feel the rewards.

But since they brought along a cameraman, the entire cast had to look their best because they were shooting behind-the-scenes footage. I also caught a cold from the gym and had to drink tons of green tea with honey and lemon to maintain my voice. I'm so glad that the work week is over and I can just rest.

I got my holiday request approved by Mr Dick and Elgin emailed me this message regarding my trip to L.A:

Hey Lezah,

I'm really happy to hear that you're coming to town. Just let me know your arrival details, I'll come see you. It'll be fun. Really excited to see you again.

Best,

Elgin

I'm really excited, too. Seeing the palm trees and feeling the warm Cali sun in the middle of the Canadian winter will be a good break. Not to mention seeing the L.A doctor again. Who knows, maybe we'll fall in love and I'll become a doctor's wife. (Who are you kidding? You hate L.A, remember?)

Chapter Eleven

Off to La-La Land!

Date: February 9, 2006
Mood: Sleepy

*I*T'S 7 O'CLOCK in the morning and I'm already at the airport nursing a nasty hangover. I am tired, but happy that I have a break from the show. I'm sipping on an extra large latte and feeling the side of my head pounding. I am not a morning person. Raleigh's with me, she's passed out in the lounge.

I didn't realize that last night after partying at Flowers Lounge that this trip to L.A was some kind of "paid holiday." What was supposed to be a quiet evening of cocktails turned into a night of wild partying. OMG, my head hurts so freaking bad; I seriously need a Tylenol.

I know I've said this before, but I will never do this again. Getting pissed drunk before taking a flight to go to on a modelling assignment is such bad business. No more alcohol! Oh man, I can't wait to get on the plane and just try to get some sleep.

Lucky for Raleigh she doesn't have to be focused like I do. When she gets to L.A, she just wants to work on her non-existing tan (she's white like Casper), do some sight-seeing and, hopefully, get laid.

All while I have to be on my best behaviour and sell product. This is going to be so much fun can't wait to see the palm trees. Landers warned me that I have to call him the moment I arrive in L.A. He's not anything to me! It's such bullocks. Not even my own father demands such things from me.

Oh, it's time to go. They just announced that flight 78 to Los Angeles is boarding. Great. More later on the West Coast; it's off to La—La Land we go!

Chapter Twelve

Going Back To Cali

Date: February 9, 2006
Mood: Content

*H*ERE I AM the ultra-chic W Hollywood Hotel. The agency has put us up in our own suites called "The Fabulous Suite." Damn, looking around here, I do feel invigorated.

After staying here for the work week, it's going to be really hard going home to a normal flat. I love it!

I start working tomorrow at 9 o'clock in the conference room downstairs. But the company I'm working for called Xentric Communications asked me to join them for a meet-and-greet breakfast at 8:15 am at Delphine. I'm really happy that I came out to L.A for this gig, the weather is great and my hang over is almost gone. Just drinking tons of water and maybe the sunshine has something to do with it. But I feel a lot better.

But right now it's only half past 10 o'clock in the morning (love how we're 3 hours back from Toronto time) and I've got tons of time to prepare for my date with the L.A Doctor tonight! As usual, I'm feeling the 'reuniting' excitement you feel when you haven't seen someone in a long time. I sure hope he still looks good.

I called Elgin when we checked into the suite and he told me that he would come by 8 o'clock to pick me up. He sounded busy and said he had to go because he was in-between patients.

I'm so hungry now; the flight was long and I just loathe that airplane food. This morning they served us with a piece of ham with a green leaf on it. I don't know what the hell that was, but I just couldn't eat it. I wanted to throw up.

I think I'll order room service and check out the extra services that the hotel offers. Wow! I feel like I'm living the glamorous life, why, oh why, do I have to go back to Toronto? Why don't I just fall in love with the L.A Doctor, quit the show and stay here forever. What a tempting thought. In L.A the sun is shining and it's only February. Why does Canada have to be so depressingly cold?

Chapter Thirteen

Mr. Chow-Wow

Date: February 11, 2006
Mood: Happy

*I*T'S ALMOST 6 in the morning and I'm already up. I can't sleep anymore. It's probably because of the butter flies in my stomach from last night's date with the L.A Doctor.

Yesterday was what I like to call my 'Welcome-Back-to-L.A' day. After breakfast, we had a Thai massage, and slept for about three hours. Raleigh went out on her own to do some sightseeing and shopping, while I got ready for my date with Elgin.

At 8 o'clock sharp I waited downstairs at the hotel lobby dressed in a little black cocktail dress from Zara. I wanted to look elegant for Elgin and let him see that I had exquisite taste. While sitting on the white circular leather couch in the main lobby, I took out my compact one last time to make sure that I didn't have any red lipstick on my teeth.

The moment I snapped it closed, Elgin walked into the lobby, we both smiled at each other and embraced. I couldn't believe what I was seeing, he was a brand new man. The man I met at my cousin's wedding was a struggling student who was stressed out and worried about finishing his residency.

Today Elgin was a fully licensed doctor and he was settled. He looked so refined wearing a black custom made suit with thin lapels and special cuff links. He was handsome as ever, as his smile, his dark hair and L.A tan made him look well-rested. I was speechless, he *looked* like a doctor. Damn, on top that, he smelled really good.

"Lezah, welcome back to Cali." He said holding both my hands while running his eyes of admiration down my body.

I did a little twirl to give him the full view and he just laughed. We hugged again and everyone at the reception desk was smitten watching us light up the whole lobby.

I was so elated I did a little dance and rapped the words of LL Cool J, "'I'm going back to Cali . . . Cali . . . Cali. I'm going back to Cali . . . yo, I don't think so. I like the suit, very nice. You're looking mighty spiffy this evening."

"Oh, this old thing? It's Ralph Lauren." He said dusting off his shoulder.

He led me out of the hotel and had the valet guy bring out the car. When his car pulled up, my mouth dropped open as Elgin's car was a black BMW X5. OMG!

He opened the door for me and helped me get in. The interior was so amazing. It was brand new and had all these buttons and features that I've never seen before. What a great first impression—a beamer.

We set off on Hollywood Boulevard and I felt like I was with the new and improved Elgin. I looked out at the bright lights of the city and seeing the palm trees on the corner streets, just made everything seem surreal.

In the car we chit chatted about my flight, his job, and my gig. He told me that he wasn't able to get the whole week off from the hospital because of the flu bug going around the schools and day cares, so he only got Friday off (which is the last day of my trip).

So our date was simply marvellous. He took me to the famous Mr. Chow's in Beverly Hills.

We sat across from another and with the dim lighting and serene atmosphere; the restaurant gave off a romantic ambiance.

I couldn't stop smiling at him, this was really him—he finally made it as a successful doctor.

We ordered sushi appetizers and our main dishes along with my favourite carbonated beverage San Benedetto (Note to self: Remember to only drink water to cure your hang over blues).

I sat there glancing away at times to take in the atmosphere while his eyes transfixed on me. I didn't feel uncomfortable knowing that when I looked away he was staring at me, I felt like he was undressing me with his eyes, but I was too shy to make eye contact with him. Instead I tried to break the ice, "So have been here before?"

"Yes, my department had our Christmas dinner party here. The food was great and I thought you would like it." He said sipping on his glass.

"I love it. I've heard so much about Mr. Chows. They say celebrities come here to eat."

"Everyone comes here to eat, it's one the most popular restaurants in L.A. Great food, great atmosphere, you can't go wrong."

I nodded, "So tell me; how do you like being a doctor?"

He laughed and I saw those two cute dimples poke through on each of his cheeks, "It's great. I really love it. Seeing those kids every day just makes my job so pleasurable."

I admired his courageousness, "I bet some of those kids inspire you, huh?"

"Absolutely! I have some patients that are so terminally ill who pull through and recover even when the statistics say they are likely to die. I don't know what it is that helps them recover; it must be the grace of God." He said triumphantly.

"Or maybe they have you, the best doctor in town!" I beamed.

He blushed, "Maybe it has a little something to do with that."

We both laughed, "But really when a child is in his death bed and the parents are at their child's side day and night, you can't help but feel their pain. Then all of a sudden when they start feeling better and we see the improvements in their health, it really is a miracle."

It was such a great night. To return to L.A and engage in such heart warming conversation with a doctor who was so handsome and compassionate, I almost came in my seamless black thong when he told me about all his cancer patients whom he helped in assisting their conditions in remission. Listening to all his stories made me feel very grateful that I was healthy and that he was indeed a passionate person when it came to his career. He really had paid his dues from the last time I saw him when he was a broke medical student who was trying to make ends meet.

Now he was doing something that he completely loved and was financially settled. The next thing that came up was his personal life; I had to ask, "when you're not at the hospital, what do you do for fun?'

"Well Lezah you know my family has always been religious, I'm still active in the church. So every Saturday I'm celebrating my Sabbath and helping out at the church."

I was really impressed. How could someone be *this* handsome, *this* smart, and *this* dedicated to the church? He really was the perfect man; perfect, perfect, PERFECT!

"That's great. I think praying and being touch with God is important in life. I'm not that religious, but I do pray and thank God every day for what He has given to me in life."

He looked at me with a twinkle in his eye, "Lezah, that's so beautiful. I do believe that through the power of prayer, all problems are solvable. Sometimes my patient's parents are at their wits end and they ask me what they should do to help their kids. I tell them to pray and some of them do and some of them don't. The ones who do pray have told me that prayer helps them cope with their child's sickness and, in some cases, prayer has helped the child's illness go away." He said proudly.

"That's got to be a great feeling for you. To help cure children is probably the most rewarding job in the whole world."

"Yes, it is. To see them smile again is simply priceless. So tell me, do you ever see yourself having any kids someday?"

"Absolutely, I love kids. I think having children is the true meaning of life and hopefully someday I would love to become a mother." I said.

Just then our waiter came and served us with our sushi appetizers, "How how about you? Do you want to have kids someday?"

"I want three of them. Doesn't matter what gender they are." He announced.

"Why three?" I said sipping on my glass.

"Three's a crowd. Since I come from a family of three kids, I want to give my kids what I experienced growing up."

"I was born on the third of July, so ain't nothing wrong with the number three."

There was a moment of silence, it was like he was dying to ask me something important, "So do you have a boyfriend? Or should I say *boyfriends* in Toronto?"

I shook my head, "Nope, I don't have a boyfriend or *any* boyfriends for that matter in Toronto."

"That's shocking. A woman like you should have tons of guys lining up to meet you. How come you're not dating anyone?"

I suddenly remembered my new year's resolution stating not to fall in love with emotionally unattainable men, "Well, the answer is simple. I just don't want to have a boyfriend right now. I'm what you like to call 'playing the field.'"

"Why?" He asked.

"I just want to be alone, it's such a liberating experience to do things for myself and not have to worry about men. I love taking care of myself."

"How long have you been single?" He asked perplexed.

"It's been a little over two years now. I was in an off-and-on relationship with that football player I told you about the last time I emailed you."

"Oh yes, I remember him. I thought you guys were broken up."

"I officially broke it off two years ago. So since then I've been completely single, no serious relationships, just having fun and focusing on my work. I'm done crying and feeling sorry for myself." I said.

He said sympathetically, "All of us have been there—lost, confused, in love and not knowing what to do. That's good you've been able to move on."

"Anyway, that's all water under the bridge. After that relationship ended, I felt like a brand new woman. I was determined to get over him, so I set some goals and now I'm having fun."

"That's a girl. So what do you think about us having a little fun tonight?"

He peaked my curiosity, "What kind of fun do you have in mind?' I said winking at him flirtatiously.

He reached out his hand and placed it on mine, "I've got something planned, something that will blow your mind."

"Mmmm, well I like the sound of that. You can blow my mind any way you like, just as long as you have me in bed at a decent hour. I've got my breakfast meeting at 8:15 in the morning." I said.

"Of course, I will not keep you out late, young lady. Your curfew is no later than twelve midnight. You have a job to do!" He said laughing.

"It's almost ten o'clock doctor, how much fun you planning to have with me?"

"It's a surprise. Something simple, but I think you'll love it." He said acting mysterious.

"I just *love* surprises. And something tells me that you're full of them." I leaned forward and placed my hand on his thigh under the table. His eyes danced as I squeezed it playfully. Screw the breakfast meeting, the night was still young and the L.A doctor has rung his bell.

*   *   *

After a delicious dinner filled with intellectual and flirtatious conversation, I kissed him on his cheek when we got back into his BMW. He blushed and I was ready to have some fun.

We drove through Beverly Hills and for a Monday night, Sunset Boulevard was buzzing with club-goers wearing their best designer party frocks and dress shirts lining up in front of The Viper Room.

"Where are we going?" I asked curiously.

"You'll see." He said placing his hand on my knee. Yes! He was finally making a move.

I noticed he was driving out of the city limits as we made our way up to the Hollywood Hills. We passed some really nice mansions and then it became dark and desolate. We kept going up these windy roads and finally after we reached what looked like the top, he parked on the side of a dirt road and facing before us was the L.A sky line. The whole city was lit up and the view was magnificent. I will never forget it.

"Surprise! Come on, let's go." He got out of the car and helped me out. We stood in front of the car and as we caught a breeze, I shivered. Elgin took off his suit jacket and placed it over my shoulders. "Thanks. It's so beautiful up here." I said admiring the view.

"I knew you'd like it." To keep me warm he wrapped his arms around me from behind. He pointed out parts of the city, "There's Santa Monica. Over there in the middle is downtown."

I turned my head to face him and suddenly our lips were so close to each other, I felt like kissing him.

He seemed keen on pointing out all the places on the sky line, but I wanted him right there. I nodded my head as he pointed to certain buildings, "You see that tall round skyscraper? That's the U.S Bank Tower. It's the tallest building in L.A."

I pretended to be listening, but the whole time I was thinking, How come he won't kiss me?

He was so focused on informing me about all the major landmarks that I sensed that he going to quiz me about the names of these buildings. I smiled and he said, "Am I boring you?"

"No, not at all." I turned around and embraced him, "You know so much about your city; it's simply gorgeous up here."

He finally caught on to the vibe I was sending him and he kissed me. I closed my eyes and made a wish. When I opened my eyes, that wish came true—Elgin, the view of L.A, the warm breeze—I haven't felt that good in such a long time. It was such a relief to be here with him in L.A. Home was so far away and this is what I needed, a distraction from the hustle and bustle of the show. Elgin's surprise was more than a drive up to the Hollywood Hills; it opened up my eyes to new ideas and made me realize that life didn't revolve around the show. I could go anywhere and do anything. The world was in the palm of my hands.

After our sexy kiss, it was almost midnight and he drove me back to the hotel. During the ride home, he held my hand at times while driving.

He acted like a perfect gentleman all the way to the end of the night when he dropped me off at the front of the hotel.

"I would invite you up, but I've got to get my beauty sleep. It's going to be a big day." I said.

"Of course, good luck. It's not like you need it, I'm sure you'll knock 'em dead."

There was a moment of that awkward silence where you want the guy to kiss you goodnight, but he's trying to find the right moment to go in for the kill.

"Thanks for dinner and the ride up the hills. It really was the perfect night." I smiled.

"You're very welcome. So see you after work?"

"Of course, I'll be off around five o'clock."

The awkward silence was there again, "So good night, Elgin."

"Good night." We locked eyes and then he finally leaned over and kissed me. His kiss was soft and gentle. I wanted more tongue action, so I wrapped my arms around him and we engaged in some hot French kissing. Wow, he sure knew how to kiss—we had some swirling tongue action that one of the valet guys spotted us and became smitten. After that kiss, I felt like I was walking on air. I went to bed feeling like a princess who had just been kissed by her L.A prince.

Chapter Fourteen

Good Gig, Bad Ex

February 12, 2006
Mood: Content

*T*HIS MORNING WAS laid back at the convention. It started off with a breakfast meeting at Delphine with the PR company Xentric Communcations. The owner is Taylor Gibson, a late-thirties PR mogul who drives a silver Mercedez-Benz convertible and looks like a true Californian. He's one of those Caucasian guys that you would accidentally mistake as a Hawaiian because of his deep tan. He knows how to talk a big game, and his success is shared with three lovely associates who he works closely with.

There's his bomb-shell assistant Natasha Stevens—a twenty-something-year-old-model-turned-PR-associate who looks like a carbon copy of Jenna Jameson with these humongous fake boobs and overly plumped collagen lips. Again, another true Californian—a hot blond with Double D's.

I also met Mark Teason—a good looking married guy (saw the ring on his finger) in his late-thirties who looks like he's Taylor side-kick *and* Natasha's lover. I don't need the proof because I've caught him a few times staring at her cleavage and licking his lips at her (massive pervert alert!).

Finally, there's Linda Moore. She is definitely a newbie in the scene. An attractive brunette and the youngest PR associate who also does a bit of their spokes modelling. She wasn't very friendly during breakfast. She didn't make any eye contact with me when she slammed a pile of press kits on the conference table. She pointed to the press kits and explained, "You have to give out one; I repeat *one* press kit to one representative to each company. Do you understand? You think you can handle that?" She said indignantly. I really don't know why she had a pickle up her ass; my guess is that she hasn't gotten laid in a *very* long time, "Yes, I think I can do it. Thanks." I muttered.

At 5 o'clock the day ends and the whole PR group takes off. Taylor says he's got some "business" to attend to while Natasha and Mark talk discreetly. After when he assists with her jacket (and looks at her cleavage *again)* they both take off together. I'm convinced they're having an affair. Then little Linda shuts down our stand and takes all the materials with her. I invited her to go for a drink at the W bar, but she just gave me the cold shoulder, "I can't. Good work, see you tomorrow."

I really like this gig, its fun and the client disappears in the evening.

So now I must enjoy L.A because it's my favourite time of the day, when work is done! So now in my suite only to find a little note from Raleigh saying that she's going to do some sightseeing. Mental note: Be sure to hang out with her before going back home. She's some chaperone, I haven't seen her since we arrived.

So get this. As I checked my cell phone, the evil ex-boyfriend called me and he left a voice mail.

"Hi Lezah, you're not answering your phone so you give me no choice but to leave you this crumby message. So I'm just

calling to see if you got my email. I haven't heard from you since we last met up, so call me back when you get this message. It's important. Take care."

What email was he talking about?

There was a second voicemail two hours later, he sounded hysterical:

"Yo Lezah, are you there? How come you're not picking up? Where the hell are you? I'm calling you because you haven't answered my email and I have to talk to you. Call me back!"

Listening to that last voice mail made the hairs on my neck stand up and very quickly I opened my laptop to check my email.

The message was sent last night around 6 o'clock Toronto time (around the time when I was with Elgin) and it said:

> Hey Lezah,
>
> It's been days since we last met and I can't get you out of my mind. I haven't slept, eaten, or done anything but laze around my apartment. I think I'm getting depressed I've lost everything that is important to me and now I have to start all over again.
>
> I am afraid that I won't be able to make it and the only thing that gives me hope is that you will give me another chance.
>
> Lezah, I still love you and I know I was an asshole to you in the past, but out of all people that I know, you understand that some people deserve a second chance.
>
> I think we deserve another shot at our relationship. I'm different now, I see things clearly and I'm ready to settle down and give you the things that you deserve.

I understand you want to be single and play the field for a while, but please think about what I said and get back to me.

Baron

Really, he is definitely obsessed. Baron has never said this to me before, he's desperate. He's acting this way because he has so much free time on his hands to do nothing but jerk off and reminisce about the past.

I looked at the email again and was contemplating if I should write him back. I sat back in the chair and decided to close the lap top and call Elgin. Screw him! I wasn't going to do anything. I let him go two years ago and I closed that chapter in my life. Baron has to accept that we are kaput.

Just when I was about to call the L.A Doctor, my cell rang and it was Baron, "Hey."

"Where the hell are you?" He demanded.

"Excuse me? Whatever happened to how are you?" I replied in a sarcastic tone.

"I've just been trying to contact you these past few days and I'm worried sick about you."

"Baron, calm down. I just read your email and got your voicemails. I'm out of town right now on an assignment."

"Where are you?"

"I'm in L.A." I said.

"L.A!" He screamed as I held the phone away from my ear, "You didn't tell me that you were leaving. What are you doing over there?" He sounded frantic.

"I told you, I'm out here on assignment." I said sternly. I was getting so annoyed because he was acting like a possessive boyfriend, and he had no right to.

"When are you coming back?"

"What's with all these questions? You're acting crazy."

"I want you to come home now!" He demanded.

"Are you kidding me? We haven't been together in over two years and you think you can talk to me this way?" I huffed.

"What about what I said in the email?"

"I read it, but my decision is still the same—I don't want to get back together."

"But I still love you."

I sighed, "Just because you say you love me, it doesn't mean that I'm going to jump back into bed with you. It doesn't work that way anymore. Baron, I don't want you anymore in my life."

"What is that supposed to mean?"

"It means that's its over! Done. Finished. Kaput! I cannot be in a relationship with you because I'm moving on with someone else."

"Moving on? Are you seeing someone in L.A?" He asked angrily.

"It's really none of your business who I'm seeing."

"Lezah can't you ever give a straight answer once in your life? Just be straight with me: are you seeing someone?"

"Yes, I'm keeping my options open. So I don't think it's appropriate that you call me anymore."

"What the hell! I tell you that I fucking love you and you do this to me? You go run off to L.A to be with some other guy?"

Calm, Calm down. My relationship hell satellite picked up one of Baron's manipulation tactic where he assumes that the whole world revolves around him. Instead of arguing with him, I just turned the other cheek, "I really have to go now." I said exhausted.

He was quiet and boiling with rage, "So that's it? You won't even think about it?"

I was beginning to sound like a broken record, "I told you, it's done! There is nothing to think about. Good bye." He was about to say something else, but I just hung up.

I paced around the suite for a moment to regain my composure. I will not let him to get under my skin; after all, I am in the City of Angels.

I was so mentally exhausted from Baron's antics that I plopped on the couch and drifted into a deep sleep with my work clothes still on.

*   *   *

Knock! Knock! I shot up as soon as I heard someone knocking on the door. The time was 8:05 pm. Shit! I had overslept from my nap and I didn't have time to get ready. I looked like a mess, still in my work clothes and felt dehydrated.

I scurried for a breath mint in my purse and checked my appearance in the hallway mirror, "One second!" I squealed. It was too late to do anything so I took a deep breath and opened the door.

It was Elgin dressed in a khaki-coloured Tommy Hilfiger blazer and dark jeans; this was definitely a more casual look from last night's date.

"Hey Elgin, come on in, I overslept from my nap." I said embarrassingly.

He walked in and had his hands behind his back, "These are for you.' He then presented me with a bouquet of red roses and I was flabbergasted.

"Oh thank you, they're so beautiful." I replied while smelling them. I couldn't believe how sweet he was. Surprise roses on the second day, he was definitely gaining points on the 'potential-boyfriend' scale.

"You're welcome." He looked around my suite and was pretty impressed, "Wow! They definitely put you up in one amazing suite."

"Let me give you the grand tour." I said putting the bouquet in a vase.

After I led him around the "fabulous suite," he sat down on the couch while I went to prepare some drinks, "Do you want a beer?" I said holding up some Budweiser.

"Nah, I don't drink alcohol. Remember, I'm religious?"

"Of course, no booze." Instead, I took out a bottle of carbonated water and poured us some glasses.

"So how was your first day on the job?" He said taking a sip from his glass.

"Great! Everything went smoothly. The PR company I'm working for, Xentric Communications, were so nice to me, well, except for one girl, I don't think she liked me very much. Anyway, I just hand out promotional items, press kits, and do a bit of networking." I took a very long sip of water to wet my dry mouth.

"Glad to hear that. Do you feel like going out tonight?" He said looking at my attire.

"I just woke up form a nap, I'm a bit tired. Is it okay if we stay in?"

He agreed to just chill out so we ordered room service and kissed on the couch while we waited to get served. This is what I needed, some love therapy from the L.A Doctor. Who needs hysterical ex-boyfriends when you have Doctor Love to cure all your troubles?

While I feasted on my Chicken Tahini, I was having sporadic flashbacks of the conversation I had with Baron. Who did he think he was? After all these years of manipulation, I wasn't going to let him ruin my assignment in L.A. I was completely in control of my life and to prove it, I was having the best time with the L.A Doctor.

Elgin sensed that I was spaced out and said, "Lezah, are you alright?"

I immediately snapped out of my gaze, "Yes, sure. I guess I'm just a bit jet lagged, I'm still on Toronto time."

"You drifted away, thought I lost you for a moment. You sure you're alright?" He asked concerned.

"Yes, I'm totally fine. I told you I'm just tired." I smiled and we both finished eating.

After rolling out the dining cart in the hallway, I slipped the 'Do Not Disturb' sign onto the door knob and we retired to my room.

I realized that I had to stop living in the past and enjoy the moment; this was something I failed to do throughout my life. And here I was with the perfect guy to start off the resolution.

We both settled on the king size bed and I took off my pants and slid underneath the sheets. I motioned him to join me and he happily obliged by taking off his clothes and revealing a very chiselled chest and six pack abs. Damn, very sexy.

We cuddled underneath the sheets and it felt so good to feel the skin-to-skin contact. God, it had been so long since I lay in bed with a really nice guy. At that moment, we passionately kissed. Our bodies naturally wanted each other and I thought there was nothing stopping us, but Elgin hesitated. When I took off his shirt, he brought up some religious beliefs and it was such a huge buzz kill, "Lezah, I like you and all, but I think we should slow this thing down."

I looked at him peculiarly and grabbed his hardness, "This so-called *thing* isn't slowing down." I giggled while rubbing him.

He blushed, "Mmmm. That feels so good, but I've got to say that this is against my religion."

"Oh come on, who needs religion when you've got a hard on?" I continually rubbed him inside his boxers.

He couldn't resist the pleasure, "I just don't want to do something that we might both regret after. Mmm, damn." He peered down at my handy work.

I decided that the conversation was over and I lightly shushed him with my finger by placing it over his lips, "Shhh! No need to talk about regrets. Let's just live in the moment." I whispered into his ear.

Right then he finally gave into temptation. I seduced him and after it was over, he held me in his arms and drifted to sleep. I quietly broke away from his embrace and saw that my cell phone had a text message alert. When I checked it, the text message was from Baron and it said:

Hey babe,

Hope your business trip goes well; let's talk about it when you get back to town. Miss you. Baron

OMG! He just doesn't get it. But on the other hand, I feel kind of bad that I slept with Elgin just to stick it in Baron's face that I'm seeing someone new. I lay in bed watching Elgin sleep and thought that life was indeed very ironic. Here I was with the L.A Doctor and my crazy ex-boyfriend was obsessing over me. How funny now that the tables have turned. Hahaha he is getting a taste of his own medicine. I fell asleep thinking Karma is a bitch.

Chapter Fifteen

Photo Shoot from Hell

February 13, 2006
Mood: Livid

$\mathcal{J}$UST GREAT! THIS trip is getting weirder by the minute. Elgin got so angry with me after the photo shoot this evening and I am clueless as what to think.

He called me out; he really just brutally told me to my face that I'm degrading myself with my job as a model.

It all started when we got into this little pow-wow after we had room service right before he took me to my photo shoot.

I was glad to see him, but he didn't seem his usual his upbeat self. Oh great, This is how men behave after they've had sex with you, I thought.

He barely said anything to me over dinner and when I told him that we had to be at the studio by 7 o'clock he murmured, "Okay, if we must."

"Is everything alright?" I said.

"Yeah, why wouldn't it be?" He said dully.

"I just get this weird feeling that something's wrong." I said furrowing my brow.

"Well, I was thinking today that we kind of rushed into things by sleeping together last night."

I knew this was going to happen, "Look, it's alright. It was great, nothing bad happened, it was just sex. Nothing is going to change between us." I said reassuringly.

"But that's the thing—sex changes everything and Lezah, you know, I'm very religious. We aren't supposed to have sex before marriage. I feel like last night was a big mistake."

Was he serious? This was the first man that had ever said this to me, "Are you against premarital sex?"

"Yes. I mean no. I mean, I'm not *totally* against it, but, ideally, I would like to have sex with the woman who is going to be my wife." There was a long pause; I felt like he was hesitating to tell me the truth, "I have to tell you something important."

I held my breath, "Yes . . ."

"I haven't had sexual relations in the past five years." He announced.

Wow. At first I didn't believe him. I was looking at him funnily, thinking that at any moment the joke would pop out of the hat. But he was serious.

"Why?" I said baffled.

"Five years ago my long-term relationship ended with a woman who I thought was going to be my wife. When she broke up with me, I was devastated. I thought we were going to get married, but she told me that she had fallen out of love and didn't want to get married to me."

I listened attentively, "Is that the last woman you slept with?"

"Yup, and after her I made the decision to practice abstinence and stay faithful to the teachings of the bible."

"When you say abstinence is that also refraining from jerking off?"

"Lezah! The church thinks that masturbation is a sin."

"Well then I'm *definitely* going to hell." I said humorously. He didn't seem so pleased.

"I have abstained from everything sexual, so that includes masturbation."

I was amazed, almost shocked that a hot-blooded man could stay away from whacking himself off, "But how do you function? Doesn't it hurt down there when you don't jerk off for a long time? I heard that men do it to relieve stress."

"There are other ways to relieve stress." He said matter-of-factly.

I was bewildered, I recalled one of my best guy friend's Darryl telling me that he used to jerk off right before a date because it relaxed him and calmed his nerves. To not jerk off for a week or so was fine, I believe that. But to not jerk off in over *five* years was simply preposterous.

"Elgin, it's totally understandable that you have abstained from sex, but to not jerk off, I highly doubt that. There is nothing to be embarrassed about masturbation, everyone does it, heck, I do it all the time." I bragged.

He glared at me, "Lezah, don't you realize that every time you pleasure yourself you're committing a sin in the eyes of the Lord?"

I sighed, "I don't believe that heresy. I think it's completely natural to get turned on. If I want to get myself off, then that's my own business, not the churches."

He shook his head, "Lezah! You mean to tell me you pleasure yourself on a daily basis and you don't feel guilty after?"

I smirked, "Never! I feel guilty that I have maxed out my Visa card and that I don't spend enough time doing volunteer work, but I never feel guilty after I masturbate. Most of the time I just like to do it so I can get on with my day."

His mouth dropped open, "My goodness that's the most deranged thing that you have ever said to me."

"Well, I guess you and I have different views on sexuality. I think it's normal to have sex and masturbate, while you choose to refrain from anything sexual. It's not the end of the world, right?"

He pondered for a moment and I had just realized that it was time for us to head to the studio. I looked at the time and it was already 6:30 pm. "We have to go now. Do you think we will make it?"

"Yes, don't worry. We'll get there on time."

*   *   *

On the way to the photo shoot, I was trying to push aside my running thoughts about Elgin's abstinence and trying to make sense as to why he really had sex with me. Did I pressure him into doing it? I quickly blocked it out of my mind as I had to do a photo shoot and focus very quickly at getting the job done. Why did this have to happen right before a photo shoot? I seriously just wanted to get this over with.

Elgin was quickly introduced to the world of photo modelling when he met the client Taylor and Natasha and the photographer Amar Ranjal. As I was getting my hair and make-up done, Elgin seemed uneasy while he sat on a retro couch looking around at all the chaos that was happening at the studio. The make-up artist Stephanie was quite chatty, I tried to keep up with her banter while she did my face, but her fingernails smelled like cigarettes and it was hard for me not to cringe.

After an hour of beautifying me, they had about five to six outfits laid out for me to wear. Two Sherry Hill dresses, two VS bikinis, and two Stella McCartney business-casual outfits.

"Lights, Camera, Action!" Joked Amar while he took test shots of me. As Elgin watched me work my magic,

Stephanie made coffee for us, and I thought the shoot was going smoothly. We did some sets where I was holding promotional items and we did a swimsuit set where I was posing on a surf board that had Xentric Communications written on it.

I tried not to look at Elgin during the shoot, but the moment he saw me on all fours on the surf board, he became enraged.

"Show me more cleavage. Push your arms together, yes, like that. Thanks." Amar said while shooting away, "Great! That looks great!" He exclaimed.

Taylor and Natasha were glancing to the notebook as the shots were being uploaded; I noticed that they were pointing and agreeing to a lot of the shots. The whole time everything was going peachy, while Elgin sulked on the couch. I really tried ignoring him because he casted a very bad vibe on the shoot.

After we went through all the outfits it was almost 11 o'clock in the evening and Amar had already taken over five hundred pictures. We all looked through the thumbnails on his lap top and I was pretty happy to see that we had a handful of useable shots.

"I think we got something here. That's a wrap!" Amar announced. Taylor and Natasha gave each other high fives and they all hugged me, except Elgin who was still sitting on the couch mulling through his cell phone.

I told him that I was done and he seemed disinterested. He barely looked up from his cell phone. I could tell that Elgin wanted to leave so we bid them goodbye.

I was happy and relieved that they were satisfied and that I delivered in a timely manner. So when we got into the car, I broke the awkward silence, "That was fun, eh?"

"Not at all. I had to sit there and watch you degrade yourself." He said bitterly.

I couldn't believe what I was hearing. Degrade myself?

"What are you talking about? I was working back there."

"Well, I don't think that being scantily clad and sprawling on the ground like that is a decent job for any decent lady." He said while we drove onto Hollywood Boulevard.

I was utterly shocked by his comments that I was speechless. Five minutes ago I felt great about myself because the photo shoot was a complete success. Now here I was feeling like a piece of shit due to his moodiness.

I let out a huge sigh and tried to keep my composure. Suddenly Elgin just snapped, "How could you do that to yourself?"

"Do WHAT?" I exclaimed.

"Do THAT! You're subjecting yourself like an object and people are ogling at you like you're some kind of sex object or something."

"Do you hear yourself right now? First of all, you've known all along that this is my job. I don't know why you're so shocked. What do you think I was doing back there? It wasn't like I was having sex with anyone."

"Well you might as well just do pornography if you're going to be half naked like that." He smirked.

I couldn't believe it; I had never heard anyone talk to me that way before, "What's your problem?" I said.

"Huh? What's *your* problem, Lezah? You're the one degrading yourself and making a living from selling your body. I think *you* should be asking yourself why you're in this business. I have an honest job, I'm a doctor."

"Oh, I get it. So it's a superior complex you have? You think just because you have this high paying job that contributes to the goodness of society you think you can belittle me, huh?" I retorted.

"I just think what you're doing is wrong in the eyes of the Lord. It's like you're a prostitute. You're selling your soul."

"What? I can't believe those words would come out of your mouth. You know what Elgin? Not everyone in the world believes in the Lord as much as you do. Just because I'm not religious, it doesn't mean that you have the right to judge what I do." I argued.

"I'm not judging you. I just think that you've made some bad decisions in your life getting into this modeling business and selling your body for the whole world to see." He said.

"Well that's my decision, not yours. I have to look at myself in the mirror every day and accept the decisions I have made, and up until this moment, I was perfectly fine it until you just freaked out on me."

We kept quiet until we finally arrived at W hotel and as I felt tears welling up in my eyes, I just wanted to run out of the car. He was so mean.

"I don't think sleeping together was a good idea, obviously, we have different opinions about things and I think you're making a big mistake in your career. I know the church would agree with me." How dare he talk this religious heresy with me? He thought that he could just belittle me because of his stupid beliefs in the church.

"I'll tell you what the Lord thinks of you now; He thinks you're an asshole. Actually, I take that back. He *knows* you're a *very* big asshole who likes to parade around with your religious beliefs and wave your superior complex in other people's faces when they remotely make a decision that you don't agree with."

"So are we done here?" He said infuriated.

"Yes, we are *done*. I don't ever want to see you again!" I exclaimed. I got out of the car and ran inside the hotel. I started crying.

Elgin just sped off onto Hollywood Boulevard leaving me waiting for the elevator feeling hot and flustered. The L.A Doctor was such a prick!

I went to see if Raleigh was in her suite, I really needed to talk to her. But when I knocked on the door, there was no answer. Great, just great, I thought.

I was furious at Elgin, how could he do that to me? I came back to my suite and took a long shower. He made me feel dirty as I scrubbed myself very hard with a towel. No one ever spoke to me in that way, not even my own father. I was so angry that I had slept with him just so I could forget about my argument with Baron. I'm such a fuck-up.

When I went to bed, I remembered my New Year's Resolution: Do not fall in love. Gladly, I hadn't fallen in love with him, but I sure was mad at myself for sleeping with him. While dozing off to sleep I thought to myself: What now?

Chapter Sixteen

I hate V-Day

February 14, 2006
Mood: Blah!

*A*RGH! WHY DO these things happen to me on the days that are about love? I completely forgot that today is Valentine's Day. I have always loathed V-day because it's just another day where mass marketing reminds all the single people in the world that they are alone. Especially after the argument I had with Elgin in the car last night, I am not in the mood for love. I just want this day to end on a good note.

I wrapped up the convention a bit early and said goodbye to the Xentric group. They were all eager to get out early seeing that they all had their Valentine's Day plans. The blond Linda was even really nice to me when she wished me a good flight back home. So I hope they all get their Valentine's wish.

While I invited Raleigh to join me for a cocktail at the W bar, we saw a lady get a Valentine's Day surprise, "Aw, look at that." Motioned Raleigh to the dotting couple, "He brought her roses. Ain't that sweet, Lezah?"

I glanced at the couple as she publicly thanked her man with a very long kiss. I was not feeling the love at all, "Yeah, yeah, they're so sweet." I said bitterly while downing my drink.

"What's wrong?" She asked curiously.

"I'm so livid right now. It's just so weird."

"WHAT?" She exclaimed.

"Elgin! We slept together a few days ago and yesterday after the photo shoot he totally freaked out on me."

Raleigh looked at me clueless, "What did he say to you?"

"Before I went to my photo shoot yesterday, he came to the hotel talking about how he made a mistake having sex with me. He told me that he hasn't had sex in over five years since his last relationship."

Raleigh almost spit out her water when she heard what I said, "Are you kidding me? He hasn't had sex in over *five* years?"

I nodded, "Yup, that's what he said. He told me that he has chosen to abstain from all sexual activity and even masturbation due to his religion."

Raleigh started laughing, "You have to be kidding me, Lezah! That's the biggest crock of shit I've ever heard. We all know that men jerk off regularly, he's just trying to put you on."

"Trust me, he's telling the truth. I do believe him because he is so religious. He told me that he was saving himself for his wife and he really didn't think that we should've had sex."

Raleigh tried to compose herself from laughing, "I'm sorry, that's just messed up. Lezah, how in God's name do you find these men?"

"Thanks a lot Raleigh, you're making it seem like I make it a habit of falling for these up-tight messed up religious zealots." I said distastefully.

"No no. I didn't mean it that way. It's just funny that's all." She said apologetically.

"Ha ha." I said sarcastically, "Well if you think that's so funny, you won't believe what happened *aft*er the photo shoot."

Her eyes widened as she took a sip off her wine, "Oh my God, I'm afraid to ask."

"Well first of all, during the photo shoot he was watching me in horror. He was sitting there looking at me strangely; I had to avoid making any eye contact with him. Then after the shoot, my God, he totally freaked out on me in the car." I paused to collect my thoughts. I was still reeling it over in my head.

"Lezah, what happened?"

I shook my head while I ran my hand through my hair, "I'm just so shaken up right now. When we got into the car, I felt like he was degrading me . . ."

"How so?" She said.

"He was mad and said 'how can you degrade yourself like that?' I was so shocked and I got defensive. But when he accused me of prostituting myself I started cursing at him."

It took a lot to shock Raleigh, but for once she was taken aback, "I can't believe he would say that to you. What were you doing at the photo shoot?"

"I wore some dresses and some bikini's, that's all. Then he starts going on about how the Lord would agree with him that I was degrading myself. I was so fed up with his religious talk that once we got to the hotel, I told him that he was an asshole." I said shaking.

"Hey calm down. It's okay. Can we have a glass of water here?" She said to the bartender.

I got all chocked up, but I held back my tears, "He made me feel like shit. I don't know what got into him." I said sipping on the glass.

"He's insane. Plain and simple, he thinks that he can judge people because of his religion. I'm so sorry Lezah, no wonder you're in a bad mood today."

"Yup, knowing my strange luck, this thing has to go down on Valentine's Day." I sighed.

"Has he apologized to you?"

"No way. I haven't spoken to him."

She shook her head in disbelief, "That's so weird. He probably has never seen a live photo shoot before and was just shocked to see you like that."

"He knew this was my job for years, so why did he have to freak out like that?" I said.

"That's the thing, he does acknowledge what you do, he just didn't know how to react when he saw you objectifying yourself."

"Well, I'm so over it. I'm *so* done with him. I like L.A and all, but I'm so glad we are going home tomorrow. I just want to go home." I said.

"I understand." Raleigh cringed, "But there is something I want to tell you, I might not come back with you to Toronto."

"Why?"

"I met someone. His name is Timmy wants me to stay here in L.A with him." She said.

"Raleigh, is that why you were out every night? You met a man?"

"Yes and he's asked me to live with him." She replied happily.

"But you barely know him and what about your boyfriend Dirk?"

"I know what I'll do. I'll call him and tell him that I got accepted into an agency and I don't know when I'll be coming back."

"But my agency is going to be pissed off at me if you don't come back, after all, they did pay for your airfare."

"Come on Lezah, they won't care about it. I'll just pay them back. Take a good look around you, *this* is L.A the land of endless opportunities, imagine, Timmy is going to become a big movie star someday and we'll be filthy rich. I'll live in a Beverly Hills mansion and sip on cocktails all day long by the pool." Raleigh said looking starry-eyed.

It pained me that my friend was so naive and that I was about to burst her bubble with my realistic pessimism, "Do you hear yourself talking right now? Honestly, you sound like a child who believes in Santa Claus for crying out loud. You're my friend and everything but you are so deluded. *Everyone* in L.A wants to become the next Tom Cruise, do you know the chances of making it big here is, literally, one in a million. It's like winning the lottery, it's virtually impossible."

"Look, Lezah just because your doctor didn't pan out, it doesn't mean that you can rain on my parade." She protested.

"I'm not raining on your parade. I'm happy that you met Timmy, but I'm just being sensible. Seriously, think about it, what you going to do out here for work? If you don't come back to Toronto with me, you'll be illegal here."

"I'll model and get a waitressing job. I've already got a place to stay and I already know the public transportation system, it can't be that hard to get a job in L.A."

"But what about money? You're low on funds and aren't you a bit weary to move in with a guy that you've just met a couple of days ago?"

"It's been *four* days!" She retorted.

"Oh yeah, my bad, knowing each other for four days is enough time to decide if you want to move in together." I said sarcastically. I had given up trying to convince her to come home, "Listen, you do what you want; you're a big girl but just be careful with him and if things don't work out promise me you'll come back home?"

"Of course, I'll come back home. But I really believe in destiny and I feel that my calling is out here."

"Sounds to me like you just want to have a party fest here and soak up the sunshine." I said lightening up the mood.

We both laughed because life was indeed ironically funny in that twisted way in that you really don't know where your destiny will take you.

After drinks, Raleigh went to meet Timmy at work. She said she would ring me later at the hotel so that we all could meet and have some drinks at the W bar.

So that means I have my last evening in L.A all to my lonesome. What's a girl supposed to do in a situation like this? Hmm, I know! It's time to whip out the plastic and go shopping!

*   *   *

I just got back from the Beverly Center and I totally lucked out. I checked out Gucci and picked up a very cute purse and I had to get a pair of these really cute black Anna Sui boots that were discounted 50% off.

After picking up the boots, I couldn't resist the temptation of some Haagen-Dazs ice cream so I treated myself after my little shopping run. While I sat on the mall bench eating a Rocky Road sundae, I saw all these couples holding hands while holding roses and teddy bears. Blah! Blah! And there I was savouring my ice cream sundae more than a man at this very moment. Who says you can't enjoy V-Day alone? Since V-Day is all about love, nothing is wrong with showing yourself some self-love.

I recalled my first New Year's Resolution: Do not fall in love. It dawned on me that this whole incident with the L.A doctor was just downright pathetic. It was probably meant to be that we just ended it this way without getting seriously hurt. I know I didn't fall in love with him, but it just sucks that he had to react that way. Oops, cell is ringing.

Oh great speaking of the devil, its Elgin, wonder what he wants to tell me?

*   *   *

OMG! He just told me that he is coming to the hotel right now! He was totally oblivious to what happened last night. I don't understand him. When I answered he sounded so up-beat and wished me a Happy Valentine's Day. Like WTF?

I think I'm dealing with another 'Doctor Jekyll and Hyde.' One day he's extremely mean and then the next day he's really nice. He practically invited himself over to my suite; I just know that when he arrives I want an apology! It's almost 10 o'clock and I've got to catch my flight tomorrow morning. Argh! These men, they really confuse me sometimes. I refuse to get all dolled up for him. On second thought, I should at least brush my teeth and freshen up my make-up, there is a slight chance that if he does apologize to me, I *might* forgive him.

Chapter Seventeen

Good Bye Cali

February 15, 2006
Mood: Relieved

*W*OW, WHAT A crazy night! It's 7 o'clock in the morning and I'm already at LAX sipping on a latte. I am so tired because last night Elgin and I had a talk about his behaviour after the photo shoot. He came to my suite all dressed up in a navy blue polo shirt with Dockers holding a V-Day gift in his hand. I didn't know what to think of it. The L.A doctor was totally oblivious. No remorse whatsoever, not one ounce of guilt of what he did to me after the photo shoot. Blah!

Before I could bring up the argument, he stuck a beautifully boxed gift in my face. When I opened the Tiffany & Co gift, there it was—a freshwater pink pearled bracelet. No doubt, the bracelet was beautiful. But I felt like he was trying to erase the bad memories from the night before by buying me some expensive gift. I was very grateful, but I don't care how much money you spend on me, I might forgive, but I certainly won't forget.

After he fitted the bracelet on me, he was full of compliments, "A beautiful bracelet on a beautiful woman. When I saw it I knew it was the one for you."

"Thank you, really, you shouldn't have." I said admiring it on my wrist.

"You're very welcome. You deserve it." He said smiling.

Honestly, I felt extremely strange accepting this gift from him, especially, after when he called me a prostitute in the car. I felt like he was trying to 'buy' my forgiveness.

I cleared my throat, "Elgin, I want to talk to you about what happened the other night."

He held up his hand in a stop motion, "There is no need to apologize. You were mad at me and I understand why you were cursing in the car."

I couldn't believe he was pulling reverse psychology on me, "What are *you* talking about? I think *I* deserve an apology. Do you remember what you said to me?"

"Not really. I just remember that you were cursing in tongues at me."

I furrowed my brow, "I was cursing at you because you insulted my job. You said I was prostituting myself. I was offended."

"Oh that!" He laughed wickedly, "I was only kidding around with you."

"That was *not* a joke. It wasn't funny at all; your words really hurt my feelings." I said looking at the bracelet and contemplating whether I should give it back to him.

"But I strongly believe that what you do for a living is immoral."

I shook my head dismayingly, "Immoral? I am not hurting anyone with what I do. What I do for a living is my own business and you're not in a position to judge me for that."

"Lezah, I didn't come here to argue. It's Valentine's Day for crying out loud! I was thinking that on your last night here in L.A you and I could . . . you know . . . ?"

"No, I don't know what you are talking about." What nerve. He looked at me with that funny look in his eyes that read "I-want-to-have-sex."

I shook my head, "Are you serious? You think that just by marching in here and giving me an expensive bracelet that I'll just forget about everything?"

"Well kind of. Take it like a peace offering."

"Elgin, we're *not* having sex tonight. If you want, I can give this 'peace offering' back to you and we can forget about the whole thing." I said in a huff.

"No, no keep it. I want you to have it. It looks so pretty on you." He said.

But I didn't feel so pretty, I felt shitty. I thought he was going to apologize and he didn't—prick!

Thinking about it now, I should have just kicked him out my suite. Tell him "I am not a prostitute!" then slap his face and he would have run away. But he insisted that we go out. So I told him that I had to meet Raleigh and Timmy at Dray's bar and he tagged along.

At Dray's, Raleigh and Timmy were totally drunk and drugged out. Raleigh told me that Timmy had scored some blow from one of his colleagues and they had been snorting lines in her suite all evening. Raleigh rolled her eyes every time Elgin spoke to us and I even nudged her to simmer down with her sarcastic chuckles.

I understood why she was staying in L.A for Timmy, he was a good-looking guy. He was a tall, slim guy who had a very perfect asymmetrical face with these big light brown eyes and brown hair. It made sense why he was an actor. He was actually a grounded guy considering he turned heads everywhere he went. Women checked him out every time he walked by them and even the gay guys were trying hard not to drool over him. Raleigh is such a lucky girl.

And here I am the pathetic working girl who hooks up with religious doctors who think I'm immoral. Geez, *why* do I have such strange luck with men?

We only stayed for a few drinks at Dray's because Elgin was eyeing me very carefully while I drank my cocktail; oh, here we go again with the judgements, I thought.

I hugged Raleigh good bye, I was really sad to leave her behind, but looking at Timmy, I knew she was going to have a good time in L.A. She's free-spirited, so I know she'll be back in Toronto someday. I just hope L.A won't swallow her up and spit her out, but who am I kidding? Everyone who comes to L.A ends up on a TV pilot that never gets picked up, then the drugs come and it's off to the Betty Ford Clinic they go. Chew them up and spit them out, *fast.*

Elgin was getting antsy and reminded me that I had to be at LAX in the morning. I think he just wanted to get me into my suite and attempt a desperate plea to get me into bed. I was so right.

By the time we got back upstairs, I hugged him outside of my room and told him that I wanted to go to bed. But he insisted that he use the washroom. So I let him in, what a big mistake.

Even after I told him that I was going to take the shuttle bus to LAX, he insisted on driving me here. So he weaseled his way to sleep on the couch. And when I woke up in the middle of the night to use the washroom, he strategically moved from the couch to my bed.

When I tried going back to sleep with my back towards him, he was breathing heavily down my neck and I felt extremely awkward. He whispered, "Lezah, I know you're awake. Oh, mmmm!" I didn't bother to turn around and face him; I just closed my eyes and tried going back to sleep. Then I felt *it*. I felt some kind of warm flesh poking me on my ass. I quickly turned on my side and saw him with his dick out.

"What are you doing?" I said appalled.

"Jerking off on your ass." He said stroking himself. Oh God. Why was I still hung up by yesterday's argument? I don't know what it was, maybe it was his creepiness that annoyed me, or if his dick was small, but I was completely turned off.

What made this jerk off session anomalous was the fact that he was saying some pretty fucked up things to me like, "Look at you glowing like Lucifer in your night gown, trying to tempt me to do evil deeds that Jesus condemns . . ." stroke, stroke, stroke, "Ah, you dirty girl you like that, don't you? Trying to make me sin against the Holy Father, making me fall at the hands of Lucifer . . ." stroke, stroke, stroke, then suddenly it happened, he exploded on my thigh.

I sat back on the bed and shrieked at the sight of his come and, immediately, I ran into the bathroom to wipe myself off. I was so afraid to come back in the room as he was still sitting on the bed.

"Hey Lezah, you can come out now!" He said tiredly. "I'm going to sleep."

I came out of the washroom and stood at the front of the bed, "Elgin, I really need to get some sleep, so if you don't mind get the hell out of here!"

He got up and pulled up his pants that were resting by his knees and let me be alone in the bed. What a relief. It was almost four in the morning and I didn't want to talk about what had just happened. It was the most uncomfortable thing I had ever experienced in my life. Kind of reminded me when I lost my virginity, that guilt I felt after the sex. But this time, I didn't even have sex with him. What bothered me was all that Lucifer stuff he was ranting about. Did he really call me Lucifer and mean it? He must be part of some kind of religious satanic cult. It was really strange.

*   *   *

I woke up at 6 o'clock and told him again that I could take the shuttle to the airport, but he pretended not to hear me. On the way there, I was quiet and barely said a word to him.

When he dropped me off at LAX, he told me to call him when I got home, but I couldn't bear to look at him in the eyes. All I could hear in my head was the echoes of what he said—all that Lucifer mumbo jumbo. He tried to kiss me, but instead I just hugged him goodbye.

Oh, just got my boarding call, flight 78 to Toronto has my name written on it. I'm so glad that I'm going home. L.A was great and all, but for now on 'The City of Angels' will be remembered as the 'The City of Lucifer.' Finally, getting out of here in one piece! See you back on the East Coast.

Part Three

Chapter Eighteen

Home, not, so sweet home

February 17, 2006
Mood: Stressed Out

*B*ACK IN TORONTO and it's just been complete chaos! There is so much to do at work. Landers has been breathing down my neck since I got back from L.A, and extremely getting on my nerves. He is pressuring me to lock in a segment this week. I have been frantically trying to organize this engagement ring segment with a local jeweller, but it's so frustrating calling the PR rep because she's always out of her office.

On top of that, Elgin has been 'virtually' stalking me with text messages, emails, and voice mails. I didn't call him when I arrived at home on Saturday evening. I just wanted to put the bad memories of him degrading me after the photo shoot and, my God, the jerk off incident at the hotel. I still have problems sleeping at night because I keep hearing his voice in my head chanting, "You are Lucifer! You are Lucifer!"

I think he is totally deranged and it's so sad that someone that deluded is a doctor. It's all just a big disguise. What sickens me is that religious people think that they can justify their evilness towards people. I understand that he was upset to see me sprawled out in a bikini on a surf board, but he didn't have to taunt me and say I was prostituting myself. Blah! Shame on him. Bad family friend.

I guess all that psychology at York taught me to try to understand people's complexities, because, after all, each and every single person is different from one another. If you show the same picture to thousands of people, each person will have their own opinions. Some people are naturally pessimistic and some people can see the beauty in the littlest things. Sadly, in Elgin's case I think he sees the images of Lucifer in me. He's got some twisted fantasies.

After several failed attempts to reach me by phone (I rejected all of his calls—thank God for caller display, don't know what I would do without it) he emailed me this weird message. Again the face of Doctor Jekyl and Hyde were written all over it.

> Dearest Lezah,
>
> It's late in the evening and I already miss seeing your sweet smile. The time we spent together was splendid; you were so gentle and sweet just like the perfect lover I thought you'd be.
>
> I am assuming it's back to the grind for you in Toronto and that's why you haven't responded to my messages. It's okay love, just call me anytime, don't mind the time difference. My line is always open for you. I was thinking of taking a trip to Toronto to come see you this month. What do you think?
>
> Love,
> Elgin

OMG! I read over this email and thought he's insane. Do you think he has amnesia? How come he doesn't acknowledge the bad things he's done to me?

Argh! But this was only the beginning of the crazy messages. The next day he sent me an email where he attached several x-rated pictures that he took of himself showing off his abs and bare dick.

I had opened his attachment at work and had to close my email very quickly when I saw his bare dick 'waving' hello at me. Just great. My mind was racing for the rest of the day; I didn't dare open the email again when I was at work. I didn't want the cast and crew to think that I was the newscaster who sat around on her break and looked at dicks all day long. So while I was shooting, I quivered a few times when I had a flashback of the pictures. I wasn't turned on; I was disgruntled the whole time that I even had to take a few breaks in between segments to erase the dick images out of my mind.

When I came home, I checked the email and scrolled through the various pictures he sent me. They were all taken in his bathroom in front of a mirror. The last ones were zoomed in on his groin and I think he even came as there was some evidence of white fluid dripping out of his dick. Wow! I couldn't believe that he would send me such raunchy pictures of himself. Whatever happened to his mighty beliefs in the church? He's such a hypocrite.

I decided to call Angela to share this berserk news thinking she would appreciate the chuckle. I filled her in on what happened in L.A—how after we slept together Elgin became crazy and started belittling me after my photo shoot.

I told her how he jerked off on me while ranting Lucifer statements.

"You have got to be kidding me. You sure know how to pick'em Lezah. We can add him to the list of mentally ill chaps."

But I dropped the biggest bomb on her, "If you think that's weird, let me send you pictures that he just emailed me yesterday."

There was an eerie pause, "Oh no. Don't tell me he's banging horses in them."

I laughed, "Oh Angela, I won't spoil the surprise. Go check your email as soon as you can. I'll send them to you now." I said.

"I can hardly wait!"

After a minute she said, "Got it. Whoa, is that come I see?"

"I thought it was only me who saw that. So what do you think?"

"I think *he* should consider a career in porn." She said laughing.

"Honestly, what do you think about his dick."

"Lezah, it looks like a hotdog with mayonnaise squirting out!" We both burst out in laughter.

"It's not as bad as it looks. But when I think about it now, I got more pleasure from using the rabbit." As we continued to laugh hysterically my stomach started hurting.

"Ah, Lezah, you're a hoot. Seriously, I can't look at these pictures anymore; they're hurting my brain."

"So do I have your approval that this situation is messed up?"

"Of course, it's deranged. Can't believe he would run his mouth on you and then send you these dirty pictures of himself jerking off! I bet he's running to every church in L.A confessing all of his sins."

"What do I do? I mean, after these pictures, he probably wants me to return the favour."

"So tell him to go watch your show!" She laughed, "I dare you to take pictures of yourself fully clothed giving him the finger."

"Actually, that's not a bad idea. But I refuse to play this kinky game. I can't believe someone would be so bold to send me pictures of their own dick."

"So don't do anything. I would just ignore him."

"That's what I've been doing and *this* is what I get. If I keep ignoring him, he might send me a package laced with anthrax."

"How about you just tell him to beat it? That is beat his dick off because he ain't gonna get any more sex for the next ten years of his life. Ha!" She exclaimed.

"Angela, that is a tempting idea but I think he needs to be reminded of how he made me feel uncomfortable. These pictures are disgusting."

"Aw, come on stop being a prude. You know you like it a tad bit, don't cha Lezah?" She teased.

"Oh frig, I'd rather go dyking it out with a hot blonde with big boobs, rather than sleep with him again." I laughed so hard that I fell off my chair.

"What happened?" She exclaimed.

I got up quickly from the floor, "Nothing, just slipped off the chair."

"Oh man, we really need to meet up this weekend for drinks. Don't hurt yourself. See you later."

Well that was it. I wrote an email to Elgin explaining to him that he made me feel extremely uncomfortable after the photo shoot and on Valentine's Day. I dared not mention the x-rated dick pictures he sent me. Just wanted to get on with it!

The next day he responded, "So I guess coming to Toronto's out of the question?" Well, duh!

Great, cell is ringing. Oh look who it is, the evil ex-boyfriend, of course.

Chapter Nineteen

Oh, What a Night

Date: February 19, 2006
Mood: Mad

THIS WORK WEEK was kind of stressful; I had more segments to shoot and was included in the Aussie version of the show. Glad Friday is here, so that means P-A-R-T-Y! So to mark the beginning of the weekend, I've RSVP at Mirage for full bottle service and Cheryl and Angela are coming. It's going to be a fun Girls Night Out.

*   *   *

By the time we got to Mirage by midnight the place was buzzing with people and the girls were ready to start drinking. Once I popped the Moet and Chandon, I had a missed call from some unknown number. Hmm, no message. Oh well, we drank the bubbly and while I sat in the VIP section, the girls were dancing and drinking with a few guys that were trying to pick them up. I stayed clear and just enjoyed the champagne. After the first bottle was finished, I went outside to smoke a Cuban cigar that Cheryl had given to me from her Santa Clara trip with Andrew when suddenly my cell started ringing. It was the person who called earlier.

"Hi Lezah, how are you? I don't know if you remember me, but I'm Baron's brother Quincy." He said.

"Oh yeah, of course, I remember you. We met at Baron's birthday party a few years back. So how can I help you?"

There was a long pause, and then I heard his brother take a deep breath, "Look, I'm really sorry to tell you this but last night Baron tried taking his own life by downing a bottle of Tylenol with a bottle of Vodka."

My legs froze. I felt so lightheaded that I feared that I was going to faint. "He did what?" I said shocked.

"He tried to overdose on Tylenol, Lezah." Quincy said with a shivering voice.

There was silence; I didn't know what to say. I really didn't think that he would do this, "I'm really sorry to hear this. Is he going to be alright? Where is he now?"

"He's at St. Vincent's hospital; they are keeping him under a 48-hour suicide watch. This morning when he didn't show up to meet me at the gym, I came to his apartment and found him lying on the living room floor passed out with the vodka bottle in his hand. So I took him to the hospital." He said shaken up.

I was speechless, I felt very ill, "Well, if there is anything I can do, just let me know."

"Well, yes, there is. I saw that you were the last person whom he called. Did you talk to him last night?"

I swallowed loudly, "Um, yeah. He called me last night and we just talked shortly."

"I don't mean to pry, but about what?"

I looked around me and for a cold winter night, there was slow traffic on Peter Street, "Baron was drunk and he told me that . . . that . . ." I hesitated to tell him the truth.

"He told you *what*?"

"Sorry, this is hard for me. Baron was very drunk and he told me that he was depressed and thinking about suicide."

"What did you tell him?"

"I told him that . . ." suddenly tears started to well up in my eyes, "I told him to call the crisis line and I hung up."

Quincy seemed upset, "Listen to me, I don't know what happened with you two, but if someone calls you and says they are suicidal you don't hang up on them."

"I know!" I said upset. The bouncer turned around and shot me a look. I mouthed 'I'm sorry' and walked further away, "I know I should've done something. But your brother is totally obsessing over me."

Again a minute silence, "Look, I know it's none of my business, I understand that you guys had a long history, but you do know what Baron's been going through lately?"

"Yes, of course. He's been released from the league."

"Yeah, and he's not taking it lightly. He worked really hard to get drafted and now that his football career is over, he's been feeling really depressed."

"So . . ." I said unknowingly, "What do you want me to do?"

"I think you should come see him. He woke up this afternoon in the hospital asking for you."

I cringed, "Really?"

"Yeah, I think you should pay him a visit and talk to him. I think he'll feel much better if you smooth over whatever issues you two are having."

"Okay. I'll do it. I'll come to the hospital tomorrow morning."

"Thanks Lezah. Again sorry to deliver such bad news, but we all need to support right now."

"Yeah, yeah. I'll be there." I said bitterly.

I hung up thinking Oh man, this sucks! What would drive him to commit suicide?

While I thought about Baron lying in a hospital bed, I smoked the Cuban cigar to regain my composure.

When I came back inside to the VIP section, I started downing more champagne while the girls were dancing with some guys to "Be My Lover" By La Bouche. I couldn't even stand straight, I felt so suffocated. My legs felt weak in my Jimmy Choo stilettos, I just had to sit down. I felt horrible about this whole situation.

Cheryl sensed that something was wrong as she plopped down next to me and said, "Hey sis, you okay?"

I shook my head in disbelief, "No, something's terribly wrong. My God, I don't even know how to say this."

Angela sat down on my right happily sipping on her drink and singing out loud to the songs playing in the club. I had this long face and both my girls were concerned, "What's wrong? You look like you've seen a ghost." Angela said.

I swallowed down on the hard lump that was sitting in my throat, "You won't believe this. But Baron tried killing himself last night."

"What!" They both said simultaneously.

"He tried overdosing on pills and alcohol. I can't believe it." I said shocked.

Cheryl's face was stunned and Angela bit her lower lip as they stared at me dumbfounded, "What the fuck am I supposed to do?" I screamed.

They both put their arms around me, "Calm down, calm down. It's okay, sweetie, we're here for you." Cheryl said.

"Do you understand now about the acts of manipulation?" I said to the both of them. They were both quiet. They knew I was totally fed up with Baron always trying to trap me into his life. I really hated to be a party pooper, but I wanted to go home. They convinced me to stay just a little while longer, while I sat on this comfy red velvet couch drinking way too much champagne while the girls danced with some guys. I felt so cut-off from our girls' night out party because my night was spoiled by my crazy ex-boyfriend's suicide attempt. Now I had the daunting task to see him in the morning. Can my life get any more bizarre than this?

Chapter Twenty

I Hate Hospitals

February 20, 2006
Mood: Exhausted

I AM SO OUT of it. I only got four hours of sleep because I tossed and turned in bed after we came home from Mirage. All night long I kept asking myself why Baron would do this. He's crazy, yes I know. But this is insane; trying to commit suicide is never the answer. I feel bad that anyone I know would ever try to take their own lives, but when it's a crazy ex-boyfriend like Baron, I have my suspicions that there is an ulterior motive.

This morning I arrived at St. Vincent's hospital at the visitor's check-in desk holding a bouquet of flowers wearing a clean pair of jeans and black polo turtleneck with my tanned UGGZ. Surprisingly, I wasn't so hung over from all the Moet and Chandon that I devoured last night.

I simply hated going to the hospital, so I also wore a sombre look on my face.

The receptionist told me that Baron was staying in room 608 and during the elevator ride up to the sixth floor, I felt sick when I smelt the aroma of the hospital which reminded me of a mixture of disinfectant and cheap cafeteria food. I simply don't like hospitals, they give me the creeps. This is where people die and it scares me.

I slowly walked down the hallway to room 608 and there he was lying in a hospital bed with his eyes-closed sitting in an upright position.

I cleared my throat, "Hi Baron. You awake?" I said standing in front of him.

He cracked a half grin on the side of his lip while he opened his eyes, "Lezah, what a pleasant surprise. I didn't think you would come."

"It's no problem. I just wanted to come by and give you these." I held out the bouquet of fresh flowers and he pointed to empty vase that was sitting on the window-sill, "You can put them in there. They're beautiful, just like you."

I grinned at him while I walked to the window and took the vase to fill it up with some water in the bathroom.

After I placed the bouquet of flowers in the vase, I placed it on the night table next to his bed. He reached out and held my wrist, "You're shaking."

"No I'm not." Obviously, I was lying through my teeth. The whole situation was nerve racking.

"So how are you feeling?" I said trying to direct the attention to him.

"Not bad. You know, my doctor keeps reminding me to take it one day at a time."

I nodded in agreement, "Exactly, just one day at a time. No need to think too far ahead."

"Who called you?"

"Quincy. He told me everything."

He looked away from me and became detached, "I wanted to die."

I reached out and held his hand, "Why?"

"Because I hate my life! When you told me that you were seeing some guy in L.A, it just killed me inside. I just started drinking every day and the thought of you with another man was fucking me up." He said looking into my eyes.

"But you have to accept that I've moved on, two years is a very long time to be broken up. Why would you try to kill yourself?"

"I don't know, everything's fucked up in my life. I feel like I've lost everything that I've worked so hard for and now I don't know what to do." He squeezed my hand tightly.

"Just do you, Baron. I'm sorry about your shortcomings, I really am. But it's hard for me to want to help you. We're adults now, but suicide is never the answer, no matter how shitty life becomes." I said sternly.

I felt awful that he tried to commit suicide, but I wasn't going to nurse him back to vitality, he needed to figure this out for himself.

Suddenly, a fairly attractive middle aged woman with long brown wavy hair came into the room and Baron said, "Hey Doc, *this* is Lezah, the woman I told you about."

"It's nice to meet you, Lezah. I'm Doctor Mary West, Baron's psychologist." She said eyeing me. Oh great, a shrink. I think I have a hunch as to what's going to happen next.

*   *   *

So my hunch was right she wanted to psychoanalyze me in the first minutes of meeting me in Baron's room.

"I hope you don't mind, but would it be possible to have a word with you in my office?"

"Sure, I guess." I said.

"Thanks it'll only take a minute. Follow me." She led me inside to her office that was decorated with classical Monet paintings on all walls.

"Have a seat." She said tapping on the antique leather chair set in front of her desk.

Just great, I just got sucked into a shrink's office. I already had an idea about what was to come.

She asked me a few questions about my past with Baron, something that I didn't like delving into. I hated reliving the past. But after some strategic prying on her part, I ended up opening up a bit about our off-and-on relationship. But she could see the distaste on my face every time she asked me to elaborate. Near the end of our little chat, she asked me, "Do you ever want to get back with Baron?"

"No doctor I have no intention of getting back together with Baron what so ever. I've already moved on. I don't mean to sound crass, but I think he tried committing suicide so that he could get my attention."

"Obviously Baron is experiencing a tough transitional period in his life and feels overwhelmed because the changes are very drastic. Most athletes and celebrities experience depression once they are out of the lime light. But he did mention to me that he still loves you and that the only reason why he is still living is because of you."

I stared directly into Doctor West's eyes, she was telling the truth, "Doctor you can't put this guilt on me. He is not my boyfriend anymore, so I don't feel that I am responsible for his actions." I said.

"Of course, you're not responsible. He admits that he is troubled. But it sounds like the pain he feels from the void in his heart is attributed to you."

I smirked, "So what are you saying? That I pushed him to suicide?"

"No, but you were one of the contributing factors that him led to it. He felt like he failed you and just wanted another chance at love." She said.

In that moment, I decided to leave. I felt as I was being cornered into some kind of ambush executed by his shrink and orchestrated by him. I refuse to get lost in this messy spider web.

When I left him the hospital, I felt relieved because I hadn't spoken about those issues with anyone in a long time. But I knew he was still trying to manipulate me through Doctor West. Thank God I didn't fall into her trap. Something tells me that she'll be a good shrink for him; maybe they'll hook up during therapy.

Chapter Twenty-One

Bad Day at work

February 22, 2006
Mood: Pissed off

*O*H GREAT, JUST great! I got into a huge argument with Landers today at work. I am probably going to get fired.

It started when he critiqued the news piece I put together after I came back from L.A on how to pick out the perfect engagement ring. I put it together, shot it, and while he was going through the final cut he called me into his office to watch it with him.

I thought it turned out pretty good considering that I put everything together in a few days. But for Landers, it was the perfect opportunity to chastise my work, "I thought it was not that bad. If I could offer any suggestions, your make-up could've been a bit thicker and you were obviously nervous. Problems at home, Lezah?"

I shot him this sarcastic look, "Not at all. Everything's just been lovely."

"Well, based on that performance I might have to re-think about adding the final cut to next week's show."

"What? But it's already done." I said.

"You look like you need a lot more practice. I'm thinking we can scrap it, and you can do another one on a different topic."

"Look, I have no problem doing a new segment for next time. But I don't know why you think it's fair that you can just cut something out from the show that's already been edited."

Landers looked tired as he had bags under his eyes and looked a bit wired, "I'll tell you *why*! It's because I'm the boss around here and I decide on final cut."

Oh here we go again, riding on his high horse of corporate power, "But the segment is good. My God, I arranged everything from writing to the shooting location. And now you think you can just tell me that you're not going to use it on the show?" I said annoyed.

"I just think that you should go out in the field and do it again. I want you to re-shoot." He demanded.

"No! I will not do it. I will not go out there and reshoot something that is already done. I'm sorry."

"Then we have a problem. If you want to keep this job, you have to do as I say." He said.

"What is *that* supposed to mean?"

"It means that the offer I presented to you that night at the premiere party is still valid." He said cunningly.

"Are you out of your mind? If you think that I'm going to sleep with you to save my job, then you can forget it!" I argued.

"Well, what do you say then?" He said utterly oblivious to what I said before.

"No way. You can just forget about it!"

"You listen to me, if you want a future on this show you will do as I say." He said angrily.

I became so furious with him that I decided to say something that was bubbling in my head for a long time, "Fuck you, Landers! Okay? Just fuck off!" I screamed while storming out of his office.

Landers stood up and yelled, "Lezah! How dare you speak to me that way! I can have you suspended from the show immediately."

"So do it! See if I give a shit if you pull me off the show." I yelled in the hallway while the whole post-production department felt edgy while they listened to our argument.

"Lezah, don't do this!" He said trying to get me to apologize.

"Do what? The last time I checked I was just working my butt off to finish this bloody segment." I walked away in a huff and retreated in the dressing room where the other ladies comforted me. They were all extremely supportive. I didn't tell them the truth about how Landers brought up the premiere party. I just told them that we argued over the segment. They understood where I was coming from. But I didn't feel guilty that I cussed off Landers, just that I publicly freaked out in front of the whole cast and crew. That wasn't professional, but Landers is such a prick.

The truth was I was mad at myself for losing my temper. With all the stress from Baron's suicide attempt (and due to the fact, that I feeling sexually frustrated), I just exploded on Landers when I was provoked. Wrong place at the wrong time. Just when I thought I could dedicate all my energy into work, his comments of something that I was proud of just rubbed me the wrong way. Now I just hope that I won't get fired. Maybe I should just apologize, oh great, I don't know what to do. Sometimes I have to learn to shut my mouth.

Chapter Twenty-Two

Greasy Chinese Take-Out

February 28, 2006
Mood: Blah

*I*N A DESPERATE attempt to try to forget about my dreadful week at work, I called Neil up to vent about Baron's suicide attempt and my argument with my power-tripping boss. So I went over to his flat and we ordered this greasy Chinese take-out food from this local joint called Abacus.

After munching on traditional Chicken Chop Soy and spring rolls; Neil popped open a bottle of Cabernet Savignon to celebrate the fact that all of his models were getting international assignments.

But who could forget about Neil's prized cash cow Anthony? According to Neil, Anthony was ringing in the big dollars, "Lezah, I am so thrilled to tell you that Anthony is in New York right now shooting the ad campaign for Rapture, CK's new cologne. Oh my God! Do you know what that means for me?" He said in a high-pitched squeal.

"Hmm, more money for your retirement?" I said sipping on my drink.

"Don't state the obvious! But this moment means something else. It means that I've made it as an agent. When I opened this agency years ago, no one believed in me. I was working out of my tiny home office and holding open casting calls in bars. I had to beg all these local designers to take any of my models for shows. And now, I am the king of the modelling world because CK is my main client."

"You are an inspiration to me." I said to Neil while placing my hand on my heart.

"Exactly sweetie. If I started from the bottom, then you have to know that you'll rise above the problems you have with work and that loser ex-boyfriend of yours."

Neil was right. If he overcame all the obstacles he faced trying to become one of the most sought out modelling agents in town, then I knew I could get through this little rut I was in.

"I know what'll cheer you up; how about tomorrow I'll throw a little dinner party at Prego, you know that Italian restaurant that just opened on King. So what do you say if I hook you up with Anthony?"

"Are you serious? You know I don't date models." I said.

"Who says you have to *date* him?" Neil said with an enticing look in his eyes, "I'm hooking you up with him for your own pleasure. You can go out with him, kiss him, fuck him, and treat him like your fantasy boy toy. Lezah, please for the love of God, do whatever you want with him!"

"You're crazy. Do I need to remind you that Anthony is a model *not* one of your personal gigolos?"

"It's not a big deal. He likes you; he said that you were hot." Neil said.

I was astounded, "You're unbelievable."

"You'll think of something later to thank me. Hell, if I can't fuck him, then I'll pass him onto you. Just promise me that you'll fill me in with all the kinky details later."

I pressed my lips, "I can't believe you just set me up like that."

"That's what friends are for." Neil said holding his glass up to mine.

"Cheers!" We squealed. Got to get a new outfit, what do you think of a CK dress and a pair of Chinese Laundry heels? Oh la la, thanks to Neil I'm meeting up with supermodel Anthony tomorrow evening. I'm so excited!

Chapter Twenty-Three

Weekend Fun

March 1, 2006
Mood: Relaxed

*S*O HOW CAN I sum up the weekend in one word? A-W-E-S-O-M-E! I am totally speechless from what happened last night.

Neil had made reservations at Prego for nine o'clock, so when I arrived Neil and Anthony were already there. There were a bunch of other attractive giraffes from Neil's agency sipping on their cocktails and mingling.

But Neil strategically had reserved my seat sitting right next to Anthony. Love him so much for setting this up. He was a perfect gentleman when he pulled out the seat from the table and once I sat down his eyes were only on me, "Hey beautiful, you're a sight for sore eyes. Glad you can make it."

"Thanks. So how was New York?"

"Good, very productive. I think today is my first day off in weeks." He said smiling.

Neil interjected, "And this will be your last. I've got you booked solid for the next three weeks."

"You sure know how to work me. Sometimes I feel like I'm a slave, instead of a model. No days offs and no edible food." We all started laughing.

After some chit chat, Anthony ordered us a round of drinks and we comfortably settled in like we were on a mini-date. He wasn't your typical egotistical superficial model; he never wanted to talk about modeling. Instead, he impressed me with his fascination with landscaping and construction. He came across as a handy man who could fix anything around the house; I liked that about him. He was versatile.

"So how's your writing coming along?" He said.

"It's going good. I'm working on TV right now, so I don't have a lot of time to write as much as I want to. But you know how it is; you have to pay your dues."

Anthony chuckled, "I know what you mean. Before I moved to Toronto I was working at this car wash just to make ends meet."

"Wow, from a crummy car wash to the international runway. Now there's a headline story right there." I said.

He rolled his eyes, "Yup. I went from living on a farm to living in Toronto. I bet by the end of the night you'll have a new story to write about. Just make sure you give me credit."

"Oh, I'll give you credit alright." We flirtatiously smiled at each other while the waiter served us with shrimp cocktail and calamari.

After the second round of drinks, I started feeling a bit tipsy. All the h'ors deurves were done and I was thinking that for a table filled with anorexic looking giraffes, they all ate a lot.

By the time our main dishes came, I had been feeling horny. Anthony was gorgeous. He had these intense blue eyes that turned me on. I crossed my legs tightly when I felt the warm wetness seeping through my panties. For a male model, Anthony had more to offer than meets the eye. The more we talked about the books we read, the movies that we hated, and the albums that we had in our record collection (yes, we both admitted to still owning a record collection). I realized that I could fall in love with him.

After dinner I pulled Neil aside and he gave me the green light, "You two go on your own way. I'm going to take these guys to Turbo for a drink and call it a night."

"Are you sure, you don't want us to come?"

"Nah, girlfriend, you *need* to get laid. Please try to relax." Neil said.

"You're too sweet, you know that? I love you."

"Love you too. You'll thank me later, just remember I want *details*. You know I'm a perv like that."

"I don't want to tell you the details of my private life." I joked.

"Aw, come on, private-shmivate. You already know that there are no secrets between us. You told me about how you slept with that European Jared in Vegas. Should I recall all the details of that sexcapade?" Neil said.

"Okay, fine. I'll tell you later. But I think I'm getting too old for details."

"Girlfriend, if you sleep with Anthony, details is a must."

*   *   *

After dinner, we headed back to his flat on King Street while Neil took the giraffes to Turbo.

The moment we got into his open concept studio flat, I kicked off my heels and suddenly I was much shorter than I appeared to be.

"Wow, you're short!" He said standing in front of me and observing the sudden height difference.

"That's why I got these." I said holding up my heels.

He held one up and observed the heel, "I'll never understand how women can walk in these. It's hard enough for me to walk in a straight line, much as less, walk in heels. It looks painful."

"Ah, that's the price of beauty: extreme pain." I said laughing.

"Sit down, make yourself at home, I'll get us some drinks." He took my coat and showed me the vintage leather couch that reminded me of a shrink's couch that patient's lie down on.

"Nice couch," I said plopping down while he went into the kitchen.

"I just love it; it's so comfortable that I pass out on it all the time."

"It totally reminds me of the couches that psychologists use with their patients." I said observing the high ceilings with dozens of halogen lighting everywhere.

"Oh man, are you going psychoanalyze me on my own couch?" He said handing me a drink while sitting down next to me.

"If you want we could have one session where I'll ask questions and you answer as honestly as you can. What's in here?"

"Vodka and orange juice, it's all I got in the fridge. Cheers!" He said holding up his glass to mine.

"Cheers!" I said as we clinked our glasses. I sipped on it quietly as he thought for a moment, "So why did you decide to study psychology?"

"No real reason. I've always been interested in people and how they behave. I remember when I was ten years old; I read this book called "Sybil" where this woman had multiple personalities. It was intriguing how she would black out and wake up in strange places. So that's where my interest in psychology started."

"When did you know that you wanted to become a psychologist?"

I chuckled, "Oh man, I remember when I was about seventeen I blurted out to some of my friends that I would be better off dead. So one of them went to the school principal and told him that I was going to commit suicide. One day I got called to the principal's office and he asked me if I wanted to kill myself. I told him no, but he didn't believe me and ordered me to see our school psychologist. I just remember when I came to see her in her office; she looked so old and bored. She didn't say anything helpful. After two meetings, I felt as if I could do a better job than her. And that's when I started to think about becoming a psychologist." I said taking a long sip from my drink.

"Why did you want to kill yourself?" He said.

"I was fed up with life."

"But why? You were only a teenager."

"Exactly. Do you remember how it feels to be a teenager?"

"Yeah sure, I felt awkward, bored, and extremely horny." He said.

"I guess boys have it different than girls. I just took everything personally and I was extremely sensitive to criticism. So I just told my friends that I felt like killing myself, it was meant for shock value, I didn't mean it."

"But you know kids take that shit seriously. That's why your friends reacted quickly; I mean if someone says they want to kill themselves, it usually means that they do."

"I know, at that time, I was just frustrated with everything. I didn't talk to my parents about how I felt, my friends were immature, and I was having an identity crisis."

"Do you still want to practice someday?" He said.

"Maybe. We'll see the state of the world when I'm old and wise. I just think that humanity is so basic and since we think we know everything, we want everything. And when we don't get what we want, we bitch and complain about our problems, and that's where the shrink capitalizes. If you're smart, you'll find solutions to your problems by yourself."

"You know Lezah, you're an interesting lady."

"I guess I should take that as a compliment." Suddenly, I turned the spotlight onto him. Talking about myself to men made me feel extremely uncomfortable." So what about you? Have you always wanted to become a *super* male model?" I said brash.

He snickered, "No way man. I believe I was just at the right place at the right time. Take a look around, this is all because of Neil's doing." He said.

"This isn't *all* of his doing; you've worked hard for this. Neil just opened the door of opportunity. I know he's proud of you."

"Thanks, but sometimes I wonder if this is worth it. Come on Lezah, modelling? When I was a kid, I used to think that models were stuck up, superficial, dummies."

"Some of them are. But you're not one of them."

"Yeah, but that's my point. I don't think I'll ever fit in with this crowd. I mean, is it me, or don't you think that a lot of these people are shallow?"

"Oh sweetie, welcome to a world where everything is about appearances, where people judge the book by its cover and are damn proud of it. If you remind yourself to enjoy the moment, then you should be okay."

"Yeah, that's what I keep telling myself when I'm prancing around in my underwear and having some fag photographer telling me to suck in my gut and flex my chest muscles."

By now our flirtatious laughter was contagious; I was lying down on the couch while I rested my legs on his lap.

I closed my eyes and felt the drunkenness seep through my body. Anthony started giving me a foot massage and it felt so good that I started moaning.

After walking in those heels, feeling his warm hands sent me to feet heaven.

Anthony showed off his massaging skills and slowly made his way up my legs. I didn't realize how much pain I had in my legs until he started massaging my calve muscles.

"I know what you can do if modelling doesn't pan out."

"What's that?" He said squeezing my right leg.

"You can become a masseuse."

"Sure and I'll just massage you every day for the rest of your life."

"That sounds like music to my ears. Mmmm." I said as he moved up my body and started to massage my inner thighs.

As his hands disappeared underneath my dress and came closer to my panties, I realized that I was already dripping wet.

I sat up while his hands were still on my thighs and that's when we kissed. I felt this insatiable feeling come over me and Anthony loved it. We both kissed passionately, while he rubbed my breasts I started to unbutton his shirt. I ripped off his shirt off and while I ran my hands over his hard chest and rock hard abs, he unzipped my dress and it fell to the ground.

Suddenly, he got up from the couch scooped me up in his arms and carried me to his bed. I remember the coolness of the bed sheets when he placed me on his bed and peeled off my bra and panties.

What continued was a romp in the sack that I'll never forget. We did it all night long. First he was on top of me, then I got on top of him. Then we did it from behind, on the side, and then on the floor. It was like high-impact aerobics except I was experiencing pleasurable orgasms.

The following Saturday morning when I woke up next to him, I thought, finally, a real man who knows how to satisfy a woman.

As I watched him sleeping, it was one of the most private moments in my life that I didn't want to exploit. I wasn't going to tell Neil about this little detail.

Being the sweet girl I was, I got up and made us breakfast. His fridge was practically empty; he had milk, a carton of six eggs and day old loaf of bread.

After having breakfast in bed, we shagged again then slept for a bit. When we woke up, he ordered two large pepperoni pizzas (our favourite kind) and after we finished it, we did it again.

I think we did it over ten times on that Saturday and I think I had over twenty orgasms. After the seventh one, I lost count and just let him do me as much as he wanted.

But I knew that this fun had to end sometime. After wilder shagging and zero slices of pizza, I left his place on Sunday morning at around 8 o'clock. He wanted me to stay with him, but my inner thighs were beginning to feel sore. The whole weekend was just one massive orgasm.

Before I left, I didn't give him my phone number nor did I ask for his. I assumed that this was going to be a one-time deal, but he told me that he wanted to see me again. Don't know if I believe it or not. It was probably just a one-night stand.

Chapter Twenty-Four

An Interesting Proposal

March 3, 2006
Mood: Surprised

*T*HINGS AT WORK are good. I thought Landers would be on my ass again, but surprisingly he's left me alone. I didn't tell Douglas about what happened. I figured that if I was going to get in trouble, I would just own up to it when confronted. But so far, so good.

Word around the studio was that my segment did air on last week's TV version. So I'm a bit confused. Did my argument with Landers scare him to change his mind and include my segment in the show? Or was this just a test?

Oh great, I feel like a total loser for falling into his trap. Maybe he already included final cut into the show, but just wanted to see how I would react to criticism. But now after I told him to fuck off, he's got every reason to get me fired.

The best thing to do is just try to move on from it and produce another segment and the next time Landers criticizes me, I'll just keep my cool and say nothing. But what if there won't be a next time? Great, cell is ringing.

*   *   *

It was Anthony and he just asked me to come over tonight at 9 o'clock. It's official—I have just secured a booty call with the male model. Considering all the shit that's going on at work, I am thrilled to have a boy toy at a time like this. He's the ultimate stress reliever. Great sex with no strings attached? I better learn to enjoy this as much as I can.

So going to slip on my black stockings and wear a sexy black garter belt and matching bra. If he's so into me the way he says, then I'm going to keep blowing his mind with sexy surprises. Got to go now and get me a piece of Anthony, grab it while it's hot.

*   *   *

Over a romantic candle lit dinner and a chilled bottle of Savignon blanc, he admitted that he didn't cook, but that he ordered in from Abacus (Neil got him hooked. No wonder the food tasted familiar).

While we ate and drank wine, Anthony brought up a riveting topic with me, "So Lezah, I want to ask you something and want your honest opinion."

"Sure." I said popping a steamed piece of broccoli into my mouth.

"What would you say if I asked you if it was cool if we became, um, friends-with-benefits?"

When I heard this, I almost choked on my food, "Are you serious?"

"Yes, I'm very serious." He said staring intently into my eyes.

Hmm, what a tempting offer. While I looked at him across the table I realized that Anthony was really hot, he did have somewhat of a brain that could hold down amusing conversations and shoot me for being a hot-blooded woman, but the thought of "bedding a supermodel" turned me on.

Plus, I wasn't looking for anything serious so, what the heck, why not?

"You know Anthony, I'm more of the relationship-type, but at the moment, I'm focused on my career so this friends-with-benefits thing might just work out for the both of us."

Suddenly his eyes lit up, "So, is that a yes?"

I bit lower my lip, "Let's just say, I want to see how things go tonight."

"You sure know how to drive a hard bargain."

"Well, I see it like test driving a car. Before you buy it, you have to try it out. If you like it, then you buy it, right?

"Couldn't agree with you more. Honestly, I haven't met a woman who loves sex as much as you do and you're just so beautiful to let go of. But at the same time, you know how it is; I'm working on the road all the time and I just don't have time for a relationship. I hope you understand."

"Of course, we're both in the biz so the crazy schedules, the constant travelling, and all the temptation to sleep with other beautiful people, it's just so hard."

He looked at me funny, "What do you mean?"

"Oh come on Anthony, don't play coy with me. Neil told me all about your sexual conquests with all the models from New York to Toronto. Ever hear that variety is the spice of life?"

Suddenly Anthony blushed as if he was embarrassed, "Well it's not like I'm a skirt-chaser. I just meet a lot of beautiful women in my job. But I'm sure you're different. I like to be taught to do things well." He said.

"Oh, it's only the beginning. I'm sure I'll be able to teach you a thing or two." I said obviously flirting.

"Oh yeah, like what?" He said taking my hand in his and leading me to the bedroom.

I sat on his bed while he took off his t-shirt and revealed his chiselled pecks and rock hard abs. I hissed, "Damn, take it all off!" And he did as I wished. After he took off his clothes, my mouth watered as I tried not to stare at his rock hard yee-haw.

When I revealed my stockings, he got on his knees and admired my legs. That's right, he worshipped my legs. I stretched them long on his bed and he kissed my legs while I spread my legs for him.

After all the leg worshipping, there was a lot of bed rocking going on as we were both dripping with sweat. Man, he took the challenge seriously because after I came the millionth time, I thought that I had had enough. But he had the stamina of an Energizer bunny. That's when I knew that we could be friends-with-benefits. I mean how could I pass up multiple orgasms with a hot male model? It's just doesn't happen to a girl like me, I'm not that lucky.

Chapter Twenty-Five

Told You So!

March 6, 2006
Mood: Surprised

*W*ELL, WELL, WELL. Guess who came home? Raleigh. Yup, I knew she would be back, I knew L.A swallowed her up and spit her out. After work I went to meet up with her at La Monde café and, apparently, things didn't go so well with Timothy (how come I'm not surprised? He's a starving actor for crying out loud!)

After meeting up at La Monde café, Raleigh looked worn out and frazzled. "So what did Timothy do?" I said sipping on my green tea.

"Timothy's a real fucking dick."

"Just tell me what happened." I pleaded.

"He hit me."

"Oh my God Raleigh, I'm very sorry. Are you alright?"

"Physically yeah. But I'm mentally messed up."

"When did he hit you?"

"Well, the first time was a few weeks ago. After doing some coke at this party, he got really fucked up. When we got home, we got into a pretty big argument because he was flirting with some chick at the party and he just bitch slapped me."

"Simply terrible. God, I'm so glad you came back home." I said relieved.

"Me, too. But now I've got nowhere to stay. I'm crashing at my Aunt's place on Dundas Street West for now. But I know I can't stay there for long."

"Just take it one step at a time. That's why it's hard when you're living with someone; you see their true colours come out."

"Yeah, you were totally right. Never move in with a guy that you've only known for a few days." We both laughed and I was glad that she was still able to see the humour in a truly serious situation.

"I only said that to you because I was trying to be a friend. You were supposed to be my chaperone while I was out there. And you just met this guy at the museum and shacked up with him right away, of course, I was going to worry about you. But I never thought that he was going to hit you. So what now?" I said.

"That's the thing, I have no plan. I have no money, no job prospects, and no place to live."

Just then I thought up the grandest idea, I would hook her up with Neil's agency. I am sure he could set up a bunk bed for her in Pussy Palace.

* * *

I am so glad it's Friday, got out early from the studio and went straight to the gym to work out and enjoy a morning of hot yoga.

So after the gym, I caught up with Raleigh for lunch at Etsu's on Queen Street and my plan worked. I set her up with a meeting at the agency, and when Neil met her he signed her on the spot, "He picked me to be his new protégé and guess what, Lezah? I'm moving into Pussy Palace!"

"Congratulations!" I said enthusiastically.

"Thanks, I would like to thank you for this; I wouldn't have made it without you."

"Wait a second there, not in the mood to hear the 'I'd like to thank' speech right now, I'm starving." I said scanning through the lunch menu.

For the rest afternoon, Raleigh and I caught up from lost time. I told her about my problems with the show and Baron's suicide attempt. In which, she was totally convinced was a desperate attempt to win me back.

I did leave one little dirty detail out and that was my arrangement with Anthony. For now, he's my little secret.

Chapter Twenty-Six

The Last Time

March 8, 2006
Mood: Lusty

*L*AST NIGHT I went over to Anthony's again (I know it's only been a few days since I've last seen him, but what can I say we're hooked)

This time it was more intense. He immediately kissed me the moment when I walked through the door. He ripped off my jacket and I unzipped his jeans. We did it on the kitchen counter, a real quickie, and after there was nothing to eat. So he ordered our usual, two large pepperoni pizzas, and we continued to do it on the couch. I can get used to this. Sex, pizza, and more sex—two of my favourite things in the world.

I spent the night and while we lay in bed he twirled a strand of my hair, I got the feeling he was 'testing' me to see if I was getting attached to him, "So are you dating anyone special?"

"Nope, not at the moment." I said.

"That's hard to believe. A woman like you probably has no problems getting men."

"I do have problems meeting men because I'm so busy with work, I'm sure you understand. It's hard to click-up with members of the opposite sex. How about you? Seeing anyone special?"

He shook his head while he smoked a cigarette, "Nope, nobody interests me. You're the only person that intrigues me these days."

"And why is that?" I said laying my head on his chest.

"You're smart and sexy. You're not like the other models I meet who are as dumb as a door knob. You have depth, something that I like about you."

He took a deep drag off his cigarette and exhaled circles with his rounded mouth, "I just wanted to know if you're seeing someone, that's all. I guess evaluate where I stand."

"Well if it's any consolation, you're the only guy I'm *seeing* and *fucking* at the moment."

He put out the cigarette on the ashtray and got up to use the loo, "That's good. By the way, you're also the only woman I'm seeing and fucking too."

I didn't want him to think that I was making it a habit of spending the whole Saturday morning with him. Even though I didn't have any appointments or anyone to see, I still got up and dressed. I just wanted to give him the impression that I was totally cool about us just fucking. You know about the whole dine-and-dash theory. You eat at a restaurant and then you take off without paying. That's the thing with this friend's-with-benefits relationship, after you have sex you leave on a high note. No fuss, no muss.

By the time Anthony came out of the washroom, I was slipping on my shoes, "Leaving already?" He said.

"Yeah, it's almost 10 o'clock and I promised my sister that I would help her out." That was obviously a lie; Cheryl was always dead asleep on Saturday mornings and didn't get up until noon.

"So will I see you again?" He said while helping me with my jacket.

"Of course, I can't wait for the next time. Call me." I gave him a quick kiss on the lips, and we said goodbye. The moment I stepped onto King Street I felt light-hearted while inhaling a gust of fresh air (even though I'm convinced Toronto's air is disgustingly polluted). Suddenly, I felt an adrenaline rush when I thought about the night I spent with Anthony. But it didn't take long to distract me when I saw a gigantic sign outside an unmarked store reading "Designer Shoes: Sample Sale 50% off" What's the one thing that can stop a woman in her tracks—it can only be shoes!

Chapter Twenty-Seven

It's Over

March 10, 2006
Mood: exhausted

*L*AST NIGHT I ended things with Anthony. I knew this friends-with-benefits relationship with Anthony was a terrible idea. Shit, I feel so stupid right now.

Once I arrived at Ultra at around 10 o'clock all prettied up in my little black Bebe dress wearing my new Jimmy Choo heels that I got from the sample sale yesterday, I spotted Neil with a bunch of giraffes at the VIP section and, lord and behold, there was Raleigh getting chummy with Anthony. WTF! They were sitting right next to each other on this black duchess sofa, looking very flirtatious.

Suddenly, I felt invisible in my new designer outfit. I wanted to hide, but it was too late; Anthony spotted me air-kissing Neil and Raleigh came up to greet me. She was already drunk as her eyes were visibly red, "Lezah! Darling, so glad you make it. Don't look now, but you see that guy that I'm talking to sitting on the couch? Well, he's a fucking super model! Can you believe it? He likes me, Lezah. He said he likes me!"

Her squeals reminded me of an annoying school girl who just found out that she made the cheerleading squad. I was speechless. I wanted to tell her, but I felt a wave of jealousy strike me in the air.

"Um, Raleigh. I have to tell you something important…" Just before I was about to break it to her that I was sleeping with the guy that she was lusting for, Anthony approached us and said, "Hey Lezah, how's it going?"

"I'm great. Nice to see you again." I said.

Raleigh shot us a puzzled look, "You two already know each other?"

"Yeah, we met awhile ago while you were still in LA." I said.

"Oh, cool." She said taking a sip from her champagne flute.

"So where's the birthday boy at?" I immediately said.

Anthony looked around the club for a moment, "He's over there!" He nodded towards a little corner where Michael Rogers, a twenty-something-year-old Nike Barbadian model, was sitting between two giraffes—African Zambi and Brazillian Leena. I waved at them, and he held his drink up to mines, "Cheers!" He hollered. Great, now that I saw the birthday boy I wanted to go home.

During the whole night, I felt like the odd one out. All these giraffes were taking pictures with Neil while I witnessed Raleigh outrageously throwing herself at Anthony. I kept trying to ignore it and enjoy the night, but something took over me—the one-eyed monsters called jealousy. From a distance, I watched the both of them in the corner of my eye getting all comfy on the couch while I kept downing all the Moet and Chandon being served by the waiters. Anthony put his arm around Raleigh and she was laughing up a storm and I kept repeating to myself We're not serious, he's not my boyfriend. But after an hour of watching my friend hook up with my current lover, the look on my face screamed: "What the fuck is going on here?"

I went to the ladies room to escape the scene and when I came out, Anthony pulled me aside near a hallway with a payphone, "Hey, you alright? You look pissed off."

"I'm not pissed off. Just tired from all that sex we had this morning, you do remember this morning, right?" I said feeling pompous.

He scoffed, "You're such a bad liar. You are pissed off. I think I know what this is all about."

"Oh yeah? So why don't you tell me." I said folding my arms across my chest.

"You're jealous that I'm talking to your friend, instead of you."

Immediately, I was appalled, "You know what, do whatever you want, don't care."

"What did I tell you when we first started this thing?" He said.

"You said you wanted to be friends-with-benefits."

"Exactly, so that means no commitments, no strings attached!"

"Okay! I get it." I said displeased, "Look, I thought I could handle it, but I can't. I'm just not built for this casual sex thing. So just do you. I'm out. Don't call me anymore." I said walking away.

"Lezah, come on." He said pulling me back, "Don't be pissed with me. We had fun, right?"

"Yeah sure, but I'm done with this thing." I said backing away, "After I left your place this morning, I felt really weird, like I wanted more from you."

He looked at me baffled, "Lezah, what do you want from me?"

Exactly, I thought, you can't expect anything more from a person you're just having casual sex with, "Absolutely nothing. I guess I'm catching feelings for you. Since this isn't part of 'the deal,' I think we should stop seeing each other."

He bit his lower lip and thought for a moment, "You sure you want to do this?"

"Yup, I just think I deserve better." I said sincerely.

He looked into my eyes and kissed me on the cheek, "So, are we cool?"

"Yeah, we're cool." I said, "Have fun with Raleigh. See ya around." Then I walked away from the super model and searched for Neil in the club. I urgently needed to talk to my BFF.

Finally, I pulled him aside after I found him posing in another impromptu photo-op, "Listen, I just told Anthony I can't see him anymore."

Neil's head shot back, "Why?"

"Because he's hitting on Raleigh and I know she's probably going to sleep with him tonight."

"So, girlfriend, join them! Ain't nothing wrong with a little ménage-a-trois." He said in his drunken laughter. Neil was totally oblivious to see that I was fuming.

"No way!" I said.

Suddenly Neil's eyes widened, "Don't even tell me that you're falling in love Anthony."

I shrugged, "I don't know what the hell I'm feeling. I just know that I don't like it."

"Girlfriend, I told you from the get-go that Anthony is only good for one thing and that's S-E-X!"

"I know! I think I'm getting emotionally attached." I said sadly.

Neil put his arm around me, "Aw, sweetie, don't be sad. It's all good, you enjoyed the sex, right?"

I nodded meekly, "Yeah, the sex was awesome."

"So be it." He said kissing me on the cheek. "Fuck it, don't worry about him. I'll just hook you up with another model. How about you just pick and choose who you want to meet and I'll set it up."

I cracked a smile, "That sounds tempting."

"Trust me, Anthony was just the beginning. I'll have more models for you to choose from and I guarantee that it'll only get better and better."

So with Neil's strange words of encouragement my confidence was up again and I was going to wish the new couple a good night. By this time, they were already making out and my presence went virtually unnoticed. So I didn't bother to interrupt them. I just wanted to get out of there. But, hey, at least I wasn't bitter.

Neil was so busy making sure that he was the divo of the party, so I left the club feeling totally exhausted and frazzled.

As I walked down Queen street on this chilly Saturday night, I realized that I'm not cut out for this friends-with-benefits thing, maybe I'm not cut out for any type of casual relationship—I'm way too jealous. But I don't like feeling jealous. But that's the thing, when it comes to the rules of casual sex relationships; can people 'turn-off' their jealousy switch?

Oh well, at least I can say that I had a marvellous time with a supermodel. On second thought, the only thing that was great was the sex. Who cares, she can have my sloppy seconds. C'est la vie.

Chapter Twenty-Eight

Not Really Friends

March 11, 2006
Mood: Worried

*S*O I JUST got off the phone with Raleigh and, apparently, after I left Ultra last night, Anthony told her that we had 'a thing'.

"Lezah, did you sleep with Anthony?"

"Yes, I did. We did it before you came back from L.A. So did anything happen with you two?" I asked holding my breath.

"I slept with him after we left Ultra. Why the hell didn't you tell me?"

"Because it didn't mean anything. It's not like he's my boyfriend or anything serious like that."

"So that's why you were acting strange. I caught you staring at us."

Only one time, I thought. "Well, whatever. I don't want to talk about it anymore. We fucked and that's it, can we just move on?"

"But why were you acting all jealous?"

"What? I wasn't acting jealous." I said defensively.

"Yes, you were! It was written all over your face."

I rolled my eyes, "Shit, shoot me for feeling a tad bit uncomfortable because I just had sex with him that day."

"You two hooked up that day?"

"Yeah, we hooked up on Friday night and I spent the night. I left his flat on Saturday morning, so when I saw *you* with him at Ultra, it felt awkward."

"But you should've said something. You should've told me."

"Like that would've stopped you from sleeping with him." I hissed.

"What's that supposed to mean?"

"All I'm saying is that you would've still slept with him regardless if I told you that I was seeing him."

"No, I wouldn't. I would have laid-off." She retorted.

"Yeah, right. Now who's bullshitting? He's a super model, Raleigh! You should've seen yourself at Ultra, you were so starry-eyed when you met him. I bet if he was married, that wouldn't have stopped you." I said smugly.

"You're so bitchy tonight." She said angrily.

"So? It's true. With your past track record: sleeping with married men and guys with girlfriends, I wouldn't put this past you."

"How dare you bring that up?" She screamed.

"Well it's the truth. From the moment I met you, you were sleeping with that Trinidadian model Ibby when he was dating that Spanish girl Christy."

"So?"

"So? Do you hear yourself right now? He had a girlfriend who *you* were friends with. And you're calling me a bitch? Girl, you better check yourself, before you wreck yourself." I said bluntly.

"Okay, so I've made some mistakes. Nobody's perfect. But it was just sex, he loved her."

"You're totally annoying me right now. After she found out that you were sleeping with him, she broke up his ass because of you. Do I even need to remind you that he gave you a STD?"

"Listen to me, I don't want to talk about this anymore, that was years ago."

"Yeah, whatever. Just stating the obvious. I have to go, I've had a long day at work and this thing with Anthony is pissing me off." I said angrily.

"Lezah, he told me that you broke it off with him."

"I had no choice! You were practically throwing yourself at him when I got to the club."

"So now it's my fault that you two stopped seeing each other?" She yelled.

"No! It's nobody's fault. I'm just an idiot for falling for this friends-with-benefits bullocks, I'm never doing this again."

"You're way too jealous. If you loosened up a bit, then maybe you could sleep with guys without any attachment. But I know you; you get all emotionally attached, when it's only sex."

"Listen to me; I've helped you land a modelling contract, a place to stay, and a guy that I was seeing. So don't call me up and chastise me. So what if I get emotionally attached to a guy I sleep with, isn't that what sex is all about? I honestly don't care about which you guys you sleep with, I'm happy for you, I truly am. The lesson here is that I'm not cut out for casual sex. I tried it, we slept together and now it's done. Life goes on."

"Okay, Lezah, cool your horses. Didn't mean to piss you off, I just wanted to make sure that you were cool about me seeing Anthony."

"Yes, I'm cool about it. It doesn't matter anymore." I said calming down. I didn't want to talk about Anthony anymore, because quite frankly, she hit a nerve. Indeed, I was jealous and very bitter that she got to him and I just let him slip through my fingers. What are the rules in a friends-with-benefits relationship? It is fine to share them with your friends?

I am not going to let this get to me. There are plenty of fish in the sea, but sadly, not all of them are supermodels like Anthony. Doesn't matter, there has to be someone better out there who will give me what I deserve. I just know it.

Chapter Twenty-Nine

Surprise, Surprise!

March 12, 2006
Mood: Happy

WELL, THAT WAS fast. Just last night I was praying that another fish in the sea would swim around and, lucky me, I got an email from Jared!

I really meant to write him, but got so caught up with work and the whole Baron drama, it just slipped my mind. Bad, bad, Lezah! How could I forget this guy who's like a slice of heaven that makes my day.

> Dear Lezah,
>
> It's been ages since I heard from my sweet angel. How is Toronto?
>
> I have some good news. I'm coming to New York in mid-April. Not too sure exactly which dates, but I know for sure that I'm coming!
>
> I'd love to see you and hope that you can make it. Write back and let me know what you think.
>
> Xoxo,
> Jared

OMG! Jared's coming to New York! I have to go see him, no matter which days it is, I'm booking it off. Wow, what a big surprise. I told him that I was going to meet him; I wouldn't miss it for the world. But I wonder what his real reason for coming to New York is? Thank God, something to make me forget about my argument with Raleigh last night. I texted her an apology and she accepted it.

No need to hold grudges with friends. Anthony's yesterday news, it must be destiny that Jared is coming to New York.

Chapter Thirty

Too Much Work

March 16, 2006
Mood: Happy

*T*HIS WEEK IS going to be hectic! The show landed a deal with UK Channel Three to shoot a behind-the-scenes documentary of what we do in and outside of the studio. Kind of like an up-close-and-personal documentary about the cast.

So the Channel Three crew arrived at the studio to start working with us this morning. They'll be with us for the week. The producer's name is Walter Birmen, a thirty-something-year-old Londoner who looked like one of the models out of a Docker's commercial. A clean cut preppy chap I must say. He brought a long two of his associates, one cameraman named Kelly and a boom guy named Charles. They were young probably in their late 20's and not bad looking chaps.

I'm super happy that on Friday, they'll be shooting me at my photo shoot that I have arranged with my photographer friend Innis Johnson. That means I don't have to come into the studio on Friday morning! Yes, thank God.

* * *

I just got home from the gym and my hour of hot yoga was awesome. I can't wait to have my beauty sleep tonight and be totally refreshed in the morning for the photo shoot.

So get this. While I was winding down my day with a cup of green tea and flipping through the pages of the new issue of "Vanity Fair," guess who rang me up? The evil ex-boyfriend did. He's back! Oh great. I had to be nice to him because this was the first time we've talked since I saw him last at the hospital.

He was in greater spirits, as he told me that he was regularly seeking therapy and was landing job interviews for various companies.

"That sounds great." I said sounding a bit more enthused. "I wish you luck with that." I gathered the courage to tell him that I had to go. Uh oh, the evil boyfriend has resurrected from the dead.

Chapter Thirty-One

Twiggy and Lezah

March 21, 2006
Mood: Content

I AM SO GLAD that this work week is over and now I can just relax and actually have some fun.

The "Night Job" magazine photo shoot with Innes was successful and the Channel Three guys came and got their footage on me. So this whole week has been a smashing success. But there was a little incident at the photo shoot involving my arch enemy Allie Gibson.

Meet Allie Gibson. She's a twenty-something-year-old model who managed to get gigs (rumour has it that she's sleeping with her seedy agent Peter Valens) and spends all her money on boozing, drugging, and partying. I like to think of her as an Amy Winehouse in the making (minus the beehive). She has a reputation of being one of the most temperamental, mentally unstable, drug addicted models in the city. I still don't know why she still works in this town; she must be sleeping with *someone* to maintain her place in the modelling world. Her look is slightly anorexic and "Toronto Life" magazine dubbed her the "Canadian Twiggy" after she was chosen as the main model for the Guess Canada ad campaigns. But the truth was, before she was discovered by Uptown Model Management, she was just working as a waitress in some local restaurant in Sudbury, Ontario.

I met her a few years ago sniffling several lines of blow at one of Neil's parties at Pussy Palace. I think she was new to the biz, and the only reason why Neil didn't accept her into his agency was because she loved to do hard drugs. She hated me instantly when we met and after I left the party she called me 'monkey lips' and said I was the ugliest Asian model she had ever seen. Honestly, I have nothing against her; I think she feels threatened by me.

When Allie made her grand entrance she went around greeting the other models, but, purposely tried avoiding me.

"Hi Allie." I said dully while the stylist placed some necklaces on my neck.

"Oh, hi. Do I know you?" She said superciliously while sniffing loudly.

"Yeah, don't you remember? We met through Neil."

"Oh yeah. You look . . . different." She said nasally. "Where do I go now? Make up? Hair? What should I do?" She yelled at the stylist.

"Go get your make-up done." Natalie the stylist said.

"No! I don't want to do that. I need coffee first, yeah, coffee!" She said storming off to the snack table.

"I think she needs rehab." Natalie said to me.

"She's already been." I smirked. Oh great, so now that my arch enemy was on *my* important photo shoot, I was worried that she was going to sabotage the whole production.

Innes was testing her camera as some of her assistants set up the props—a purple velvet couch, champagne flutes on a marble table, and a bottle of Don Perignon chilling in a silver bucket.

By the time all five models were fitted with their outfits, Allie was refusing to wear any purple eye shadow, "I have green eyes. Can't you fucking see that purple eye shadow doesn't highlight my eyes?" She argued with the make-up artist.

"But we're using the same make-up on all the models. You're going to have to suck it up." She said.

"No! I want to use my own make up!" She screamed. The make-up artist just sighed and walked away.

Minutes later, Innes came to Allie and talked to her sternly, "Listen Allie, I came up with this great idea the other day that I want a purple theme. I want a very funky look like what "Purple Rain" projected. Do you know what I mean?"

"Ah! Okay, fuck, fine. I'm only doing this for you because you're my friend. But with any other photographer, I wouldn't wear this stupid shit around my eyes." She muttered.

Innes slightly shook her head while she walked away.

Just then, I saw Charles the Boom guy and cameraman Andrew walk into the bar heading to my make-up station to greet me. I introduced them to Innes and they gave her a run down as to what they were going to shoot. While the guys were setting up, Allie yelled, "Why is there a film crew here?"

"They're here for me." I said proudly. "They're shooting a documentary about me."

"Huh? *You*? You got to be kidding me." She said aloof.

"Actually, I'm not kidding. Why, are you jealous?" I said coldly.

"You bitch!" She shrieked.

Everyone gasped while I rebutted, "Allie, why don't you go the ladies room and stuff more blow up your nose. It's what you do best."

"Shut up! You shut up! You don't deserve a documentary about your life. If I had known that this photo shoot was going to be about a dumb ass Asian model with monkey lips, I wouldn't have accepted this assignment!"

"You listen to me, you strung out junkie! Shouldn't you be in some alley way shooting up right now? You're lucky that you're still working in this town. If you don't want to be part of this photo shoot, then get the hell out of here. As the famous saying goes, 'the show must go on.'"

"How dare you talk to me this way? Who do you think you are? You're just a stuck up bitch who strips on the internet. You have no talent; you don't even know how to model."

"Oh really? So I guess showing up to a photo shoot all coked out and yelling at everyone is the professional model behaviour?" I said blotting my lipstick with a tissue while the other models were quietly chuckling.

"You're nothing! I'm calling my agent to tell him that you're harassing me."

"Okay, you do that sweetie. Just remember Sniff! Sniff!" I said mocking her.

"Bitch!" She screamed getting up from her make-up station.

The moment she stormed off, everyone let out a huge sigh of relief and the rest of us chit chatted about the weather and which new pair of shoes we were eyeing at Aldo. It seemed that all of us were fully aware of Allie's high-strung outbursts and for some strange little reason some of us were a little amused by her coked out tantrums. I wasn't amused, I was simply annoyed. My tolerance for washed up models was diminishing. But since this was *my* day, I wasn't going to let our Twiggy model addict get in the way of the photo shoot.

After two hours of hair and make-up, all five of us were ready to shoot while Innes was in the washroom having a little pep talk with Allie. The Channel Three guys were already shooting behind-the-scenes footage while I got chummy with the one male model that I was going to pose with. Innes had her own vision as to how she wanted this editorial to look like, so she positioned each one of us on the plush couches and she had me sitting on top of this cute male model named Brennan holding a champagne flute. My job was seduce to him while the other models wore their masquerade masks and simply observing us.

"Okay, so is everyone cool with what I want? I want to see the ladies stand tall, suck in your guts and push out those butts. It's shooting time!" Innes announced as she positioned her camera.

"But what should *I* be doing?" Allie said lighting up her cigarette.

"Just smoke and look pretty on the couch." Innes said. "Lezah, I want to see those bedroom eyes while you look at Brennan. Like play with him, tease him and you Brennan, I want you to look deep into her eyes and pretend like you're falling in love with her."

"Nice." Brennan said looking at me while Innes took some test shots.

"Just relax." I said putting my hands on his chest, "It'll be fun."

"Sure!" He said in a high-pitch squeal.

While Innes was shooting us, the guys were also filming the photo shoot. In between takes Cameraman Andrew took the opportunity to ask me a few questions, "So how are you feeling about the photo shoot?"

"I think the photo shoot is going great. Innes is one of the best photographers I've worked with so far, she's got so many brilliant ideas and the other models are fantastic, except for one who doesn't take her job seriously. But I am not at liberty to say who it is; everyone here knows who I'm talking about."

"Oh, I see. So do other models get catty with each other or are all of you friends?"

"Sometimes, you might click with a few models and hang out. But most of the time, we're all just acquaintances. Some personalities clash because of big egos and drug use, so from time to time a model will get catty with me, but I don't let it bother me. I just laugh it off. I'm here to work and at the end of the day, it's not about me, it's about the final product."

"Ha!" Allie shrieked in the background while still lying on the plush couch sniffing loudly.

I just ignored her while Andrew asked, "And Lezah which do you like better: modelling or TV?"

"That's a tough one. I like both, but if I had to choose, I like TV better because I have a voice and can express my opinions."

"Ha! I don't think stripping in front of a teleprompter is legit acting." She hissed to everyone.

"Will you just shut up?" I said glaring at her. The cameras were still rolling and I seriously wanted to smack her.

"No! I don't want to be part of this documentary!" She screamed at Andrew when he aimed the camera on her.

"So get out of here!" I screamed.

Suddenly Innes interjected, "Ladies! That's enough. Lezah and Allie, I don't want you in this shot. So Allie take a break and go get some coffee. Lezah, please get your make-up touched up. I only want Natalie, Brennan, Taylor and Jessie in this shot."

I went to the make-up station and flopped down on the chair while the guys followed me with their camera, "So Lezah what was that all about?"

"Well, Allie isn't the most professional model to work with." I said while the make-up artist applied a coat of lipstick to my lips. "Can you guys stop filming, please?"

"Sure. I think we've got everything. Is everything alright?" Andrew said putting down the camera.

"Yeah, everything is good. If you guys got everything you needed, can we wrap up here?" I said politely. After reviewing their footage, they agreed to finally leave. I wish they could've stuck around a bit longer, but Allie was making me nervous. She was obviously trying to ruin my show, so I had to get them out of there.

In that afternoon, Allie went to the bathroom a total of twenty times! For a girl that size, she sure as hell does a lot of coke. By the time we wrapped up it had been almost 6 o'clock and all of the models started leaving. While Allie was lying on the couch she was ordering drugs on the phone, "I'm out. I'm done a photo shoot; meet me at the same time, same place. Yeah, same thing. Bye."

While I studied her frail frame, I realized that she was severely anorexic. Her wrists were small and her ankles looked wobbly. I was just going to leave without saying goodbye to her, but I couldn't resist, "So take care Allie. See you."

"See you." She murmured under her breath while looking at her cell phone.

"You know, you look so skinny. You sure look like you can use a sandwich." It was then that I tossed her a left over sandwich that catering had left for us to eat during our break.

She screamed at me, "You bitch!"

I shot her a smile while she was furious. I walked out of Zizi bar feeling resilient and victorious. It was a good day at the office, very much indeed.

Part Four

Chapter Thirty-Two

Canned!

March 27, 2006
Mood: Angry, but relieved

I CAN'T BELIEVE IT, Landers just fired me! I know it's because I told him to bugger off the other week. What a schmuck.

He called me into his office this morning and I assumed he wanted to talk about the photo shoot documentary. I took a deep breath when I knocked on his door as he sat staring blankly at the computer screen.

"Hey Landers, you wanted to talk to me?"

"Yeah, can you close the door?"

As I shut it, he leaned back in his black leather swivel chair and collected his thoughts.

"So what's up?" I said while I sat down.

"Well, let me just start off by saying that you have done great work for the show this past season. Even though I think you still need to improve in some areas, overall, the fans like you." He paused like he was changing gears and that uncomfortable silence that I felt with him at our last meeting was very much alive again.

"So with that being said, you know Lezah, we have a lot of fans. Each lady on the show attracts all kinds of viewers to tune into the show. But lately, our ratings have dropped slightly and the producers are looking to make some cut backs." Pause again. I was thinking Awkward feeling please go away!

"So what are you getting at, Landers?" I said a bit dumbfounded.

Landers shifted in his seat, leaned forward and folded his hands together, "There is no easy way to say this, but, after careful thought and consideration Douglas and I have decided to release you from the show."

OMG! The awkward feeling turned into a surreal moment that made my mind space out and ask, "What?" I asked in a state of shock. "Why are you releasing me?"

"It's because of our budget. We have too many ladies on the roster and as you know, we hired you on as a co-star. Douglas feels bad that he has to let you go, because you're the newscaster with less sonority, so you're the first to go. I'm sorry Lezah, but this decision is final and we have decided that we don't need you on the show anymore. So you're fired." He said calmly.

Those words you're fired. I loathe those words, especially when you're not expecting to hear it. In that brief second, I had a flashback on everything that I did on the show. I never called in sick, I never missed a segment, I was always on time, I showed up to every event we had to promote, I followed the rules, and I even did the extra segments and Irris' photos shoot. And *I* just got fired? It just didn't make sense to me. I tried to stay calm, but I could feel my eyes water and my heart beating faster. "You know what? I just thought about my performance on this show, I showed up on time to all my call times, I did everything right, and now you're telling me I'm getting fired? I'd like to know for *what* reason?"

"As I said before, it's due to our budget. You know our ratings have suffered . . . ."

"I don't give a shit about the ratings! I want to know why I'm getting fired!" I yelled.

"This is why Lezah! You have a very bad temper and after what you said to me last month after I was just critiquing your segment, I had a little talk with Douglas after and he said swearing at me was totally inappropriate. Not only was it unprofessional, but it was highly disrespectful. Douglas wanted to fire you then, but I saved your ass and told him to give you another chance."

I scoffed, "Oh give me a break, Landers! Do you think that I actually believe you that *you* gave me a second chance? Let me remind you that the only reason why I cursed at you is because you were blackmailing me to sleep with you."

"Ah Lezah, that's why you should've given us a chance." He said cunningly.

"You're sick, you know that? You guys just used me, you had it all planned out. You didn't *save* me from the show; you just wanted your footage for the UK documentary."

Silence again. This awkward silence was annoying me, I wanted some damn answers. "There is another thing." He said.

"What?"

"Well one day Douglas and I were reviewing some of your latest segments, and we both agreed that you have gotten bigger since you started on the show."

"So what are you saying?" I said looking at him suspiciously.

"You're gaining weight." He snickered.

Wow! What a low blow. I hate it when men judge women by their weight. It's no wonder so many women have eating disorders; he made me feel so worthless, "What a cheap shot. You fire me and tell me that the reason why you're letting me go is because I'm getting fat?"

"Look, you can think whatever you want, but you were lucky that we kept you on the show, do you know there are thousands of women out there who want your job?"

"I can't believe all this bullocks. Completely unbelievable! If there are thousands of women who want to be on this nude internet Mickey Mouse show, then go fucking have them! Now that I'm fired, let me just say this one thing. This show is a big farce! Since day one I've been feeling that this show isn't going to get me anywhere in my career."

"Then do something about it!" He exclaimed, "My God Lezah, if you feel this way, then go out there and make it happen! A lot of our past newscasters have done well after they have left the show." He said.

"Landers, don't try to lessen the blow, I am not a stupid girl. You guys were just waiting to fire me after the documentary wrapped up."

"Lezah, you're acting irrational. I told you it was because of the budget."

"Budget, smudgette! First it's the budget and then it's my weight. If you call this a TV production, you can do a lot better than that." I huffed.

Suddenly, Landers face became pale as a ghost, "Lezah, again I'm sorry we have to let you go. That's how it goes here, it's just show business."

"Show business? You're going to stoop that low and say that I got fired because 'that's just show business?' This show ain't nothing about show business, it's a joke, do you realize people out there are laughing or jerking off to us? Do you want to know why this is so hilarious?"

Landers stared at me blankly, as if his lips were frozen due to fear that I was going rip his head off if he spoke up.

"It's funny that you're firing me off a show that I think is a complete waste of time. To come to think of it, I don't need to strip on the internet to become famous, you guys can shove it! Because finally I can say I am free, I can do whatever I want."

"Yes, yes." He agreed meekly as if he just wanted me to get out of his office.

"So is this my last day?"

"Yeah. I'm sorry, the decision is final. We didn't schedule you for any segments next week, but we'll still pay you two weeks salary."

"Wow, talk about kicking me to the curb." I said shaking my head in disgust. "You guys have a lot of nerve treating your newscasters like this. You don't see us as talented individuals. You'll see what I'm going to do after the show." I warned him.

"Lezah, I do wish you the best of luck. Sorry the show didn't pan out for you. But I think you have potential to become something great."

"Yeah, thanks. I'll get my things." And that was that. I was done with the show. That's life for you. Ain't it funny? One day you've got a job and then the next day you're fired and collecting unemployment checks.

I left his office in a huff and slammed the door so loudly that a blonde guest model shuddered while waiting in the reception.

"Asshole!" I muttered underneath my breath as I made my way outside to the car parking lot.

I sat in my car and while I started up the engine, I couldn't concentrate to drive. My hands were shaking, I was so livid.

I replayed what was just said in Landers office and I couldn't believe it, I had just gotten fired.

I thought I wanted to cry, but I couldn't do it. Instead, I screamed at the top of my lungs and punched the steering wheel a bunch of times while some passerby's witnessed me going temporarily insane.

After throwing a fit, I looked at myself in my rear view mirror and said, "Calm down! It's not the end of the world." I could feel some pain forming all around my head and suddenly I had a splitting head ache.

I still couldn't drive, my hands were still shaking. Everything was a sham. The whole show was a sham. My whole life stood still and in that moment, I was done. Well now at least I can go to New York.

But what now? I kept asking myself over and over again. What the hell do I do *now*?

I couldn't think straight. My mind was racing a mile a minute; I didn't want to tell anyone just yet. What the hell was going to happen to me?

I decided to do my usual routine and go to the gym and take a yoga class. Yes, yoga will make me stop shaking! After the shaking ends, I just want to drink. Now that I'm fired, I don't have to be anywhere, so that means I can do whatever I want. I'm thinking a lot of alcohol this weekend.

*   *   *

The good news was my hands stopped shaking after my yoga class. The bad news is that I'm still having trouble accepting that I'm now officially unemployed. So to celebrate my firing, I passed out on the couch after drinking half a bottle of red. When Cheryl came home she woke me up and I told her the terrible news that I had just gotten fired.

"What?" Cheryl shrieked.

"Yeah, unbelievable, but it's true. Landers sacked me this morning. He told me that today was my last day on the show."

"But what was the reason?"

I shrugged, "Apparently, they can't afford to pay my big fat ass. Landers told me that I was gaining weight."

"Oh my God, that's just straight-up rude."

"Yeah, I know it's a bunch of bullocks. But I know the real reason why I got fired it's because I didn't sleep with my boss."

Cheryl just stared at me with sheer disbelief in her eyes, "Are you serious?"

"Yeah, I am. He hit on me months ago before he was promoted at that season premiere party we had. I refused him and when he became the boss we butted heads."

My sis sat next to me on the couch and put her arm around me, "Maybe this was meant to be. I always thought that you were too good for that show. You don't need it in your life." She said.

"Exactly. So instead of crying and feeling sorry for myself, I just want to do nothing."

"Are you sure you're feeling alright?" She said putting her hand on my forehead, checking to see if I had a fever.

"Yes! If this was any other job, I would be devastated that I got fired. But for once in my life, I feel free. I feel like a weight has been lifted from my shoulders." Hmm, life after "Barely a News Show," what am I going to do now?

Chapter Thirty-Three

Who is Duke Silverston?

March 28, 2006
Mood: Confused

*S*O LAST NIGHT I went over to Neil's flat to tell him the news that I was officially fired from the show and he comforted me by popping open a perfectly chilled bottle of Chardonnay. Ah, that's what friends are for.

While we were sitting on the couch, we were looking through some of my photo albums on Facebook. I showed Neil the Vegas album where Jayden and I were together, "So that's him. Ain't he sweet?" I said smiling at Neil.

"Um, yeah. He's hot." He looked closely at the screen at all Jayden's pictures and reluctantly scratched his head.

"Do you need glasses? Why are you looking so close?" I said.

"Um, Lezah, I know this is going to sound crazy, but I think I've seen him before."

"Where?" I asked puzzled.

Neil looked me straight in the eyes, "Lezah, you won't believe it when I say this, but I think Jayden's a porn star."

I laughed so loud, "Nah silly, I mean don't get me wrong, he is handsome enough to *be* a porn star, but he's not the guy you're thinking it is."

Suddenly, Neil took over laptop, "Listen, sweetie, I'm going to Google his name right now it's Duke Silverston. I swear it's the same guy that you met in Vegas and the one that I've seen in pornos."

So while Neil searched on the internet, I took a long sip of Chardonnay when suddenly I saw a naked picture of Jayden pop up on some adult magazine website and that's when I nearly spat out my drink, "Holy shit!" I gasped, "Is that really *him*?"

"Oh hell yeah, that's totally him." Neil said clicking on each and every thumbnail revealing close ups of Jayden's private parts.

As I stared at each different picture of him naked, both frontal and back, I just went into a state of denial. I knew it was him, but somewhere in the back of my mind, I was telling myself that they were two different people. I needed to snap out of it, "You know what Neil; I bet this isn't really him."

"Ah, no you didn't! You can't be that blind, maybe you're the one who needs glasses. Just look at all these pictures; I swear to God it's him."

I took one closer look at our Vegas pictures with me and him locked in an embrace than compared it to the naked pictures on internet of him flexing his muscles and baring his erected dick for the whole world to see. It just seemed like a long stretch, I remember him telling me that he worked in film production; nowhere did he mention porn in his job.

I thought back to those nights we spent together, and I remembered how his naked body looked next to mine when we were in bed all those hours and, suddenly, there was no turning back. I came to the conclusion that, yes, the naked male model on the internet was the guy I slept with in Vegas. Whoops. Like a really big Holy-Shit-Whoops.

Neil went to another website called Beautiful College Boys and there he was topless promoting the site as a featured model, "Girlfriend, he's the biggest gay porn star in the whole world."

I still didn't register in my head that Jayden was not only a porn star, but a *gay* porn star, "Neil, I don't want to hear this right now."

"So do you believe me or not? It's the same guy; I'll never forget a man that looks like that."

"I can't believe my luck! Of all men I hook up with in Vegas, I end up sleeping with a guy who is a gay porn star. How messed up is that?" I said conflicted.

"Calm down, stay calm, my Bella." Neil said rubbing my shoulders, "It's not that bad, I mean he is hot. I am sure he also likes women, I mean, look at you! Girlfriend, I even told you that I would sleep with you if I wasn't gay."

"Oh Neil! This is just terrible. I still don't want to believe that that's him." I said pointing to the nude pictures on the laptop.

"Do you want me to shed more light on this situation?" Neil said reassuringly.

"How?"

"Let's watch all his movies. I have them on DVD." He said getting up while opening his DVD case.

I stared at him mortified, "You mean to tell me that he did more than *one* movie?"

"Girlfriend, he's a global sensation. Just drink more and I'll put in a movie."

"No, we're not doing this." I said dreadfully.

"Yes we are. We are going to drink and smoke while we watch your boyfriend make history."

I screamed while I held the sofa pillow on top of my face, "No!"

"Lezah, stop hiding underneath there. Come on."

This was getting weirder by the minute, "I can't believe you have all these movies. I can't believe he's the star." I said flipping through all of them, feeling awkward about the whole damn thing.

"So let me just say that most of his movies are my favourites, so which one you want to watch? This one's pretty good, 'Duke Silverstone's Summer Holiday.'" He said holding up a DVD with some blonde Eastern European guy embracing Jayden on a beach.

"Neil, this is awkward. Just pick anyone you want." I said feeling nervous.

"Hmm, well it's a hard choice. I like this one because he does it on a bus. But in the other movie, he is on top. But the birthday bash is better because there is an orgy. So . . ."

"For the love of God, just pick one!" I screamed feeling impatient.

"Okay, girlfriend, don't get diva on me!" He said doing his signature two snaps in a circle move.

"Did you just say orgy?"

"Yeah, since it caught your attention, let's watch this one." Neil handed me the DVD cover of "Duke Silverston's 21st Birthday Bash" and there it was my life going to change right before my eyes.

We started smoking while Neil played the DVD. I wasn't in the mood to see his acting skills, so I ordered Neil to fast forward straight to the sex scenes. I had to see if that was really him with those men.

"Lezah, let's try to watch all of his acting scenes so you can appreciate his whole career."

I looked ghastly at Neil while I handed him the smoke, "You can't be serious. How many times have you seen this movie? Let me guess, about one hundred?"

"Um, no. My estimation is thirty to forty times."

"I bet you have jerked off to this video, huh?"

"Yeah, sure. But I have other jerk off favourites."

"So just fast-forward it!" I demanded. And fast-forwarding is what Neil did. When we got to the sex scenes, I watched Jayden perform various lewd acts on men including receiving and giving blow jobs while the plot was about the preparation of Duke's 21st birthday bash at some hot weather resort.

At first, I was a bit uncomfortable. I had never watched a gay porn before, this was the first one. But when I saw Neil's expression on his face he seemed so engulfed in the gay sex that Jayden and some other European model were doing, I felt kind of cool that I had met such a sexually charged man. But while I was watching Jayden in a twenty man orgy, I thought it was sick, but on the other hand, it kind of turned me on. It was like this erotic, illicit world that he was in. It was hard to believe that was the same man that I spent four days with in Vegas. Completely two different people.

After the movie, I felt confused about everything. Neil asked me if Jayden had told me about his porn job. I thought about everything we talked about in Vegas, he told me that he worked as an editor for a production company. Great, it's probably for the same production company he acts in.

"I'm still in a state of shock. I mean, we just watched the movie and that's *him*. I know it's him. It's so strange to see him doing that because I was with him. I don't know what to think."

"It just means he's bi-sexual. You can handle that, right?"

I shook my head in disbelief, "I never slept with a bi-sexual man. This is all new for me." Again, my headache was throbbing.

"Girlfriend, millions of women sleeps with bi-sexual or gay men, they just don't know it. It's completely normal, I mean with so many men on the planet and fewer women, it's bound to happen that men are going to sleep with men and women at the same time."

"Neil, sometimes your world views are so fucked up, I don't know what to say."

"Say you'll not freak out over this? Promise me, you are still going to see him in New York."

"What? I can't think straight right now; I don't know what to think about all this!" I said holding up a bunch of his DVD's in my hands.

"You need to talk to him about it. He probably has a clear explanation as to why he is doing these dirty movies. It's probably for the cash."

"Neil! I don't think he is going to have a scholarly explanation as to why he's doing some guy up the butt in the movie."

"Maybe he's not gay. You know in the biz there is a saying about guys like him; they're only 'gay for pay' or 'gay for cash.'"

"Oh come on, that's not true. No straight man can be gay for cash."

"You are so naive about the gay porn world. Didn't you know that these gay porn stars are fathers, husbands, and boyfriends in relationships with women?"

"That's great! But I don't want to be one of them." I said.

"And why not?" Neil boasted.

"Because, Neil! It's just not what I pictured in my mind about a devoted husband and father. Can you imagine if I had a child with him? What would we tell the child? 'Your Daddy pays for your college tuition by doing it up the butt with other men.'"

"Why can't you just meet a man and have fun with him? Why does it always have to lead to marriage and a family?"

"Because, unlike you who just wants to do it up the butt, I want to meet a man who wants to get married and have a family someday."

Neil said rolling his eyes, "But Lezah, you're too young to get married. Plus, I don't want you to get married."

"Why not?" I said shocked.

"Because the moment you get married, you'll turn into one of those Married Snobs who forget all about their single friends the moment they say 'I do.' I *know* I'm still going to be single and then you'll pity me and I'll die alone crying in my sleep holding a bottle of vodka on my chest."

"Stop being a divo, Neil. How do you know you're still going to be alone in the future? How do *I* even know that I'll ever get married? And even if I did get married, I would never stop talking to you, you're freaking hilarious and you just unravelled this messed up situation that I now I have with Jayden."

"Oh yeah, of course, we got off topic again. Look, it's not a big deal that your *potential* husband is a gay porn star."

I almost laughed, "You're just saying that because you wish you were me."

"Think about it. He makes good money, he's internationally famous, and he's hot. In the gay community, that's the ultimate catch."

"Sweetie, good point but I am not in the gay community. How can I describe it? I just think that if he's a gay porn star, how could he be attracted to me, a woman?"

"Now here we go again. For someone who writes about sex and relationships, you have to open up your mind in accepting different kinds of sexualities. As you told me before you've experimented with women, so what's the big deal if your boyfriend is bi?"

"Neil, fine. I get it; he's a bi-sexual. It's just not the thing I wanted to find out tonight, especially, after I just got fired."

Suddenly, Neil felt sorry. "I know girlfriend, today's been an awful day for you. You sure know how to pick 'em."

"Told you, it's my strange luck, I get fired from a TV show and just found out the guy of my dreams is an internationally famous gay porn star. Yup, that sums up my life for you. I have to talk to him about this. I have to hear it from his own mouth, and then I'll decide if I still want to go to New York."

That night I crashed on Neil's couch and woke up in the middle of the night thinking to myself "Is this a problem?" After that I fell back to sleep feeling that my life was deeply troubled.

Chapter Thirty-Four

Long-distance Calls Sucks

March 29, 2006
Mood: Confused

*A*FTER NOT SLEEPING so well last night, I couldn't wait anymore. I called Jayden long-distance in Europe. I didn't know which was more shocking. Getting fired or finding out that a lover of mine is a gay porn star?

When he answered, my heart dropped, hearing his voice sounding so foreign, so different, and so far away. I almost forgot what to say to him when he asked me why I was calling, "Listen, I don't know how to say this, but yesterday I got fired from the show."

"Oh love, I'm sorry to hear that. But I know you're clever, you'll find something else." He said cheerfully.

"That's not the main reason why I'm calling you; I have to ask you something important."

"What is it?"

"Um, look, it's something odd and I don't know if this is a good time to bring it up." I suddenly tensed up and hesitated if he was Duke Silverston, legendary gay porn star.

"Oh, Lezah you can tell me anything. What is it?" He repeated.

I sighed, "Okay, here's the thing. One of my best friend's Neil is gay and yesterday while I was hanging out with him I told him that I got fired and that I was thinking about coming to see you in New York."

"Aw, I see. What did he say about you coming to meet me?"

"Well, that's the funny thing. He thinks it's a lovely idea, he is happy that you invited me there. But . . ." I paused and tried scrambling for the right words to say, but I just hesitated.

"Lezah, you're cutting out. Are you still there?"

"Yeah, I'm still here. Jayden, this is hard for me to tell you, but Neil showed me something about you on the internet yesterday."

"What did you see?" Jayden asked perplexed.

"I saw you naked on the internet you were posing on these *gay* porn sites. Then Neil told me that you were a porn star." I paused to hear the reaction that I was oh-so-dying for—shock or denial. But instead he just laughed. It was a nervous laugh. What the hell did that mean?

"Ah, Lezah. You've got some friend there." He commented.

I wasn't too pleased with his answer, "So after Neil told me this information about you, I didn't believe him, so he showed me a movie. We watched one called 'Duke's 21st Birthday Bash.' Am I making sense?"

Then there was an uncomfortable pause on the phone. I felt pretty nervous by this moment.

"Jayden, can you just say something? I mean, is that really *you*?"

I held my breath for his answer. This was the defining moment when I wished I wasn't repeating images of the twenty man orgy scene in my head, "Yes, Lezah, it is true. That's me."

OMG! Hearing him admit it to me was shocking. Up until that moment, I was holding on to that 2% chance that maybe it wasn't him. That maybe he had a long-lost twin wandering aimlessly in the world that just *happened* to become a gay porn star. I was speechless.

"Lezah! Are you still there?" He said.

"Wow, I feel like someone knocked the wind out of me. Jayden, why?"

That's when I heard Jayden's voice change, it became lower and serious, "Lezah, it's a *very* long story. I meant to tell you, but I just didn't know how."

"Now ain't that the truth? It's not one of those things you talk about on the first date. Imagine if you told me this when we just met in Vegas? I would've been long gone."

"Exactly, that's why I didn't tell you! If I had told you about this life I had, you would have just left me."

"So you just lied to me to get into my pants?" I said.

"No! I didn't lie to you. I just didn't want to scare you away. When I met you, I wasn't thinking about my past."

"You know, I've met some messed up people in my life, but you take the cake. But in Vegas, you were you. I just don't understand."

"Exactly, you didn't meet Duke. You met me—Jared! It has nothing to do with my past. I was planning to tell you if you came to New York."

"So what are you going to do in New York?" I suddenly got the dreadful feeling that he was going to tell me that they were going to shoot his next movie called "Duke Silverston Does NYC."

"I'm doing a photo shoot." He replied.

Bingo! Great, that was just great. In his world, a photo shoot meant that he was naked sprawled on some cabana chair jerking off. I suddenly became curious, "So is this photo shoot like the stuff that I saw on the internet?"

"No, no. This is better. I'm going to be in a coffee table book about porn stars."

Wow, I bet his parents would be so proud. Imagine coming home to Mom and Dad and giving them a coffee table book with you inside showing off your wiener for the whole world to see? Again, I was speechless.

"So a coffee table book, huh? Is this going to tasteful nudity or just straight-up raunchy ass shots with whips and chains?" I said trying to lighten up the mood.

It worked because we both laughed, "Sorry to disappoint you but there won't be any whips and chains, it will be tasteful. I wanted you to come with me to the photo shoot. I want to introduce you to the photographer and the whole crew."

"Oh no Jayden, that's not necessary. I don't want to get in the way and, plus, it would be weird for me to be there."

"Why would it be weird? Didn't you just work for a TV show where all of you were naked?"

"Yeah, that's true. But I don't know about seeing *you* naked." I said.

"Holy shit, do I look that bad when I'm naked?" He joked.

"I didn't mean it that way; I just need some time to take this all in that's all."

"I know. It's not easy to hear this news. How do I explain all of this to you in a long-distance call?"

Suddenly, I just wanted to get off the phone and think about everything, "Listen sweetie, I have to think about it."

"Think about what?" He said.

"Jayden, I just found out that you're a gay porn star! It's not that easy."

"Lezah, you're mistaken. I *was* a porn star, I am retired."

"Okay, this is too much for me right now. I have to go, I'll message you soon."

"Please don't be mad at me, love." He said sweetly.

"I'm not mad; I just need to be alone right now." I said.

And alone time is what I got. After we hung up on the phone, I felt relieved that the truth was out; Jayden was, indeed, Duke Silverston. But I was also confused. The people who knew he was a gay porn star would call me his 'cover up' girlfriend or worse his fag hag that he occasionally shags from time-to-time. Would they ever think I was his girlfriend, considering that he's doing these guys up the butt in all these movies?

Argh! My mind is racing one mile a minute. Why can't I just fall in love with a normal guy who works a normal job, has a normal apartment, drives a normal car, and leads a normal life? I wanted to forget about him and move on, but I couldn't. There was something strangely attractive about him. Come on, let's be real who you fooling? It's because he's a European man who just happens to be quite smashing in bed. Other than that, he's one of the nicest people I've ever met.

But you know what's so bizarre? Neil was right; there are probably tons of women who are married to these gay porn stars. But how do they not freak out? Who in their like mind would want to marry a gay porn star?

I wish I could talk to one of these women who are involved with these kinds of men. It's probably weird. I wonder if there's like a 'gay-porn-star-wives-and-girlfriends' club where everyone meets up once a month, smokes and sits around drinking coffee and eating sandwiches, while they share their thoughts and issues that they have with their gay porn star husbands. Hmm. Is this even something I should be thinking about? Yes! In this messed up world we live in, it *has* to exist.

Chapter Thirty-Five

No Where to Go

April 1, 2006
Mood: Bored

I MADE UP MY mind today. I am going to New York. But I must emphasize that there is a very big 'but!' I must keep up with my new year's resolution that I can't fall in love with anyone. This trip should just be about schmoozing, shopping, and sleeping. And if sex should unravel between me and Jayden so be it. *But* I am not going fall in love!

I swear this was the worse timing to get fired. I don't know what to do with myself. After watching Maury Pauvich, Jerry Springer, and Oprah I get the impression that the outside world is more messed up than mine.

Probably the real reason why I'm talking so much nonsense is because I've been drinking and smoking every day since I got fired. So this is what it's like to be an unemployed bum. Everyone's at work, cocktails at noon, and Special K for all meals. Oh man, I better go to New York.

* * *

It's only 2 o'clock and I literally watched a bunch of "E! True Hollywood" stories on Jennifer Lopez and Angelina Jolie. Now I'm trying to look for jobs on monster.ca; it's so hard to concentrate.

My God, after a week of being unemployed what else is there to do after reading magazines, masturbating, and snoozing?

I have to get of this flat and do something with my life. So I'm heading out now to shed some lbs at the gym, then I'll stay for yoga after. Hmm. Maybe I can apply at the gym as a yoga instructor, but don't I need a certificate for that? Oh God, this is a sign of desperation, I'm thinking about teaching something that I'm not even qualified in. The things we'll do during tough times.

Chapter Thirty-Six

Too Drunk To Care

Date: April 7, 2006
Mood: Still bored

*A*FTER A WEEK of not working, I am settling quite well into my life of leisure. So to celebrate the weekend, I took Angela and Cheryl out to get wasted so that I didn't have to feel bad that I've been boozing this whole week by myself.

So get this, last night while we were partying at System's lounge I got a text message from Baron saying:

What's up Lezah? Haven't heard from you in a while, what you doing tonight?

Oh great, this ex won't ever go away. I was so drunk and having a good time that I didn't bother to reply. But after we left System's, he texted again saying:

Hey did you get my last message? Hit me up, I'm thinking about you.

So in secrecy while Angela and Cheryl went to fetch something to eat at the hot dog stand, I replied with a drunken text:

Hi Baron, on the street now with the girls, how are you?

After I texted him back, I tripped on Richmond Street while I ate my hot dog. With my drunken state and uneven stiletto heel, I fell face forward as my half-eaten hot dog flew out of my hands and plopped onto the ground. Cheryl and Angela both lifted me up and dragged my ass into a taxi cab. I kept chanting, "My hot dog! I can't believe I dropped my hot dog!"

Suddenly, I was so drunk that my head began to spin. I felt nauseous (probably from the hot dog relish that tasted rotten), so I stuck my head out of the window to breathe in some fresh air. Within this buzzing daze, Byron texted me back saying:

I'm not doing so well. I miss you. Can I come over to talk?

What does he want to talk about now? I'm so talked out! But you know when you're so wasted you have what I like to call "A Momentarily Brain Fart" when you just don't give a shit about what's going on. So I had a change of heart with Baron, I do admit that I've been extremely bitchy towards him. With the whole failed suicide attempt, do I have to be so cruel? But what do you expect? I'm his ex!

So when we got home, I waited for Cheryl to go to bed and I texted him back giving him the green light to come over and talk.

I couldn't tell Cheryl that Baron was coming over, she would totally freak out. She calls him Mister Rhino because she thinks he resembles a rhinos aurous.

While I l poured myself a cold drink of vodka and orange juice, I started dozing off on the couch when he arrived at my flat.

When I opened the door, I caught a whiff of his strong Armani cologne as he reached over to hug me.

"Hey! You got here so fast." I said.

"I had to see you, urgently."

"Well come in, make yourself at home. Cheryl's in bed so we have to keep things down." I said as I poured him some water.

"You're drunk, aren't you?" He said sitting down on the couch.

"Yeah, a bit. We went out to party tonight on Richmond; I'm celebrating my new life." I blurted out.

"What's your new life?"

I paused and stood tall, "I got fired from the show."

"Why?"

"Because of my weight. They think I'm turning into a big pig."

"That's ridiculous. You're not fat. You were too good for that show anyway."

"Thanks!" I said feeling a bit better, but still too drunk to erase the post-firing shame that most people feel after they hit the bottle.

Blame it on the alcohol but I caved in to what Baron probably wanted for a long time—a romp in the sack. As we undressed each other while leaving a trail of our clothing from the couch to my bedroom, oh great, if sis wakes up before I do, she's going to know that we slept together.

But it was just a random hook up with an ex, so it doesn't matter. But I will not allow myself to fall back into our dysfunctional relationship because this was just a one-time tryst. This doesn't count.

*   *   *

After we shagged, he wanted to sleep over, but I just kicked him out. I knew Cheryl probably heard the sounds of my bed banging against the wall, so she probably figured out that I had some late night booty call with *somebody.*

When I got up, Cheryl was sitting on the couch flipping through the pages of "Cosmopolitan" while sipping on some coffee. When I muttered good afternoon to her, she barely looked up from the magazine, "So . . . how you feeling? Do you have a hang over?"

"Yes. My head is fucking killing me now, I need a Tylenol." I said sifting through our medicine cabinet.

"So . . . something strange happened this morning. When I got up to use the washroom round five this morning, I saw Baron, naked, in our living room picking up his clothes from the ground." She said finally making eye contact.

I didn't know what more was embarrassing, that my sister saw Baron naked or that she just right-handedly caught me screwing my crazy ex-boyfriend.

"Um, I can explain. You see, last night he was texting me when we left System's, remember in the cab?"

"Uh-huh." She said.

"Look, I told him that he could come over to *talk* and, you know, I was drunk and horny and one thing led to another . . ."

"Lezah, you *fucked* your ex-boyfriend who you hate!" She exclaimed distastefully.

"I know what I said. But you know. I slipped. Okay, so I know I made a mistake by sleeping with him, but shit, I'm only human. I have needs to."

"So if you have needs, why couldn't you hook up some random guy at System's, you didn't have to get back with your ex."

"Let me set the record straight. We are *not* back together. We slept together this one time, but that's it. It's a one-time deal." I said.

Cheryl rolled her eyes, "Now I've heard that before. I swear to God, if you get back with him you're crazy."

"I swear to you, I will *never* put myself through this hell again. I had a moment of weakness, come on, will you just lay off? I just got fired, and shagged my ex-boyfriend for the hell of it. I am not the first and the last person on this earth who had sex with an ex."

Cheryl rolled her eyes again and sighed, "Just remember the way he treated you when you two were together."

"I know. Don't worry, I have everything under control. It was just a booty call, nothing more. I don't even like him anymore." Just then I realized it was the perfect time to tell her that I was going to New York this week to be with Jayden. Oops, Jayden. How could I be so stupid?

"Listen, I am not getting back with Baron because I have some good news for you."

"What is it?" She said with anticipation in her eyes.

"Do you remember that European guy I met in Vegas, Jayden?"

"Yeah, what about him?"

"Well, he's coming to New York this week on a business trip and he invited me to come join him."

"Wow! That's awesome. What's he doing in New York?"

I also realized at that moment, that I shouldn't overwhelm Cheryl with all the dirty details about Jayden's past. She was still getting over the shock of seeing Baron naked in our flat today, so I needed to lessen the blow bit-by-bit, "He's coming to do some work for the week and during his off-time he wants to spend some time with me."

"So do you think he likes you?"

"Yeah, of course. I dig him too. That's why I'm going to see him. I think he might be someone special." I said.

Cheryl and I grew silent for a moment. I felt guilty that I just had sex with my ex and was setting off this week to New York to meet Jared. Is this slutty behaviour or what? If you think about it, I am free to do whatever I want.

* * *

After I unsuccessfully scanned through the Toronto Star classifieds, there was nothing that I was qualified for. So many sales manager and customer service positions were available, but I just wasn't motivated to apply. After dashing the paper in the trash, I called my Mom and Dad to tell them that I had gotten fired. They weren't surprised, Dad just advised me to keep looking for a new job while Mom sounded a bit relieved, "Maybe you can find a job related to your education. How about going back to school to finish your Masters?" Yeah, I wish I had the discipline to go back to school. But I don't want to, I feel like my calling is somewhere else. Now that the show is over, I hope that my relationship with my parents can get better.

After getting off the phone with Mom and Dad, I read online that I'm having a quarter-life crisis. God, if things are this bad at 27, imagine when I'll be 47 and on menopause?

Suprisingly, there were no obsessive text messages or phone calls the next day after my impulsive drunken shag with Baron. I'm still kicking myself for sleeping with him. But I know that after sleeping with him, I don't want to be with him. I want to see Jared in New York.

So check this out. When I was got home from the gym, Baron was waiting for me outside of my building. Talk about stalker! How long was he waiting there? What if I got into a car accident and was hospitalized, would he still be waiting outside my place?

I wanted to avoid him, but it was too late. He followed me in the lobby and joined me in the elevator.

"What do you want?" I said as the elevator made its way up to my flat.

"I want to talk to you."

"The last time you said you wanted to talk, we ended up shagging in my bed. So I hope you came here to talk because we're not doing *that* again." I said.

While we got off the elevator and made our way to my flat, he grabbed me in his arms and tried to kiss me, "Stop it, Baron!" I said pushing him away.

Once we got into my flat we stood in the foyer, "So why did you come here? There is nothing more to talk about." I said folding my arms across my chest.

"So the other night meant nothing to you?"

"Oh for fuck sakes Baron, it was *just* sex. Why can't you get it through your thick skull?" I said annoyed.

"Because I thought that you were giving me another chance."

"That's the problem; you still want us to be a couple. But I'm moving on, I don't want to be with you anymore."

"So what about the other night?" He said.

"I still feel the same; I'm not in love with you anymore. And I know this kills you, but I'm involved with someone else."

"Who is it?" He demanded.

"Some guy from Europe."

"Europe? Are you serious? You're involved with some Russian?" He smirked.

"He's *not* Russian! He's a very nice guy from Slovakia." I said confident.

"Ha! Sounds like a jerk to me. All those Euro trash guys only use women for sex; you think he's going to marry you?"

"This is not about marriage! This is about moving on with life."

"Fine, go be with your Russian. You know, I think you're making a big mistake."

"First of all, drop all this Russian shit. He's not even from there."

"Oh yeah, so where is he from? What do you even know about this guy?"

"He's from Slovakia and he's a decent man." I said proudly. I was very annoyed and decided that it was time to say goodbye.

"Lezah, this guy sounds shady. But it's up to you. What can I do to convince you to stay?"

"Absolutely nothing. I want you to leave me alone."

Suddenly, I felt a bit sad because I knew that this was truly the end for me. I knew I would never see him again.

There was no goodbye hug or a goodbye kiss, only a wicked good-bye that I would like to forget, "So now that you're going to New York, I have something to tell you."

"What?"

"Me and five other guys are going to Aruba next weekend for a five day holiday."

"So what, is that supposed to make me jealous?"

"No, it just means that I was playing you all along. I never wanted to get back with you; I just wanted to see if I could get you into bed one last time before my trip to Aruba."

"Get out! Get out of my house!" I screamed opening the door. "Remember this Baron: when you come back from your trip to Aruba, I'll be long gone. You'll never see me again." I slammed the door so hard on his face that I could still hear him breathing heavily on the other side.

"Lezah, you're making a big mistake!" He yelled while he knocked on the door.

"Just leave me alone!" I screamed. I couldn't even cry anymore because it was just so pathetic. Reminder to self: Say hell no to ex-boyfriends and hello to new lovers. The lesson learned: Never *ever* sleep with obsessed evil ex-boyfriend no matter how drunk you get.

Chapter Thirty-Seven

Last Night in Toronto

April 19, 2006
Mood: Content

*I*T'S MY LAST night in Toronto before I head to New York tomorrow so Neil invited me over to chill. After ordering pizza (finally, not that greasy Chinese food) Neil and I discussed my thoughts about the trip.

"My God, I must be insane for going to New York tomorrow." I said.

"Girlfriend, trust me, he's going to be on cloud nine when he sees you."

"I know things are going to be great when I get there, but what's bugging me is what am I going to do after this trips done?"

"Are you talking about your whole jobless situation?"

"Yes, after the show I don't know what to do with myself. I don't want to jump back into modelling or acting. I'm so sick of the whole biz, everyone's fake, producers are assholes, and the good work is scarce. What am I going to do?"

"Why don't you ask God for answers?" He said sympathetically.

"I do! Every day, every minute, every moment that goes by I keep asking God what am I going to do with my life. And on top of that all, last Sunday I slept with Baron because I was so fucking drunk."

"You did *what*?"

"I slept with Baron after I got totally wasted at System's on Saturday night."

"What possessed you to do that?" He said.

"I was drunk and pissed off that I just got fired. Just feeling shitty about my life, I guess."

"Oh Lezah, he was such a dick to you." Neil said.

"Okay, so I had a moment of weakness. We slept together once! Shit man, it's not like I committed a crime. Anyway, after sleeping with Baron, I know it's officially done."

"So in Lezah's picture-perfect world, what do you envision?" Neil said engulfing a pizza slice into his mouth.

"I envision getting up every day, writing, reading, sleeping, eating, working out, and cooking. And sex if I can manage it."

"All in that order?" He laughed.

"Yes!" I smiled, "It's my dream. But what if I told you that I honestly want to go to Europe with Jayden?"

"I would say go! If this is what you really want, then go to Europe. It can be truly liberating."

"So you don't think it's far-fetched if I want to go with him back to Europe after New York?"

"Nope, not all. I think you should do it. For the love of God, just do it!" He pleaded. "This is the opportunity to see the world. But first you have to get along completely and feel love for each other."

"Yeah, I know what you mean. What if he finds me extremely repulsive? Imagine, we're going to be together for five days in Manhattan, what if he thinks that I'm bitchy?"

"You bitchy? Never."

Part Five

Chapter Thirty-Eight

Going to New York

April 20, 2006
Mood: Excited

*G*OOD MORNING DIARY, I'm on flight 88 to La Guardia in New York. This mission is do or die. Ha! I'm so excited to visited New York again, this will be my twenty-something time going there. Other than that, I think I'm insane (or just totally bored out my wits) for meeting up with Jayden. Why do I always do these crazy things? I must be Miss Desperate. Or maybe I could fall in love. Not. As all my friends say, I sure know how to pick 'em.

I'm scheduled to arrive at LaGuardia in one more hour, and my hands are shaking. Shit, I have to constantly use the loo. I can't eat the disgusting airplane food because I'm afraid I'll just puke.

Before I boarded the plane, Jayden sent me a text saying:

Hi, love. I arrived last night in New York. I'm at the condo now; you're going to love it. Can't wait to see you at the airport. Have a great flight. Xoxo J

I can't believe he is coming to pick me up at the airport! I haven't seen him, in the flesh, in nearly two years. I read in the morning "New York Times" that it's going to be a lovely day at the stock market, dow is up +4.

And now I'm here on this flight, totally 'up' for this weeklong rendezvous with this guy from Bratislava. To come to think of it, I don't know where that is in Europe. I'm pretty sure it's in the former Eastern Bloc. I should find Germany on the map and if I look close enough, Bratislava can't be that far away. This trip is going to be different, international espionage, maybe he's a double agent working for Eastern Europe filtrating the States, gathering information, all while disguised as a gay porn star. Who am I trying to fool?

I'm just freaking out a little because the man sitting next to me stinks, I don't think he's showered. Gross. Get me out of this plane!

But what if there's a Vegas curse? Just because you get along with someone in Vegas, it doesn't mean that you'll get along anywhere else in the world. Knowing my strange luck, he'll probably loathe me after a week together and then he'll flat out dump me before he goes back to Europe. Or maybe I'm just freaking out because this guy freaking stinks! I'm going to the loo.

*   *   *

Finally, we are landing in thirty minutes. I have now resorted to covering my face with an airplane blanket to mask that nasty funk that guy is wreaking with. I'm sure other people can smell him.

Anyway, last night before I left Neil's flat, he gave me a little gift—a charm bracelet. I am wearing it now. He said that he barely gives women jewellery, but this was good luck for me. I was very happy, "Thank you, Neil. I love it. I'll be sure to wear it everywhere."

"Lezah, if you do go to Europe, please let me know." He said getting teary-eyed.

"Come on, no crying!" I pleaded. "I'll see you again soon. You're acting like I'm moving away."

"It's okay, let me get emotional. My shrink says that I have problems expressing my real emotions, so here's some practice. You'll call me when you get there?"

"Yes!" I said holding his hand. "You're acting like my mother."

"That's good; I'll tell my shrink that I expressed my emotions like a mother. She'll like that."

"I'm going to miss you." I said reaching out to hug him.

"Me too. You'll always be my bella. So knock 'em dead grab New York by the balls and say 'I'm here to take a big bite out of the Big Apple!'"

After he embraced me, Neil said, "Remember I am living vicariously through you, so please whatever you do: fuck the porn star!"

Those were the last words he uttered to me and now it's all I can think about. Damn him. I'm cursed. Fifteen minutes.

Chapter Thirty-Nine

The Big Apple

April 20, 2006
Mood: Happy

*N*EW YORK IS fantastic! Arriving at La Guardia was surreal because it's been something I have been fantasizing about since I got fired. Then to see Jayden, I mean, how else to say it? It felt like a modern-day fairy tale come true.

When I arrived at the airport, all my anxieties melted away the moment I spotted Jayden sporting a dark blue Polo jacket waving at me through the crowd and holding a bouquet of red roses. I guess that's when I entered a state of shock because I said aloud, "This never happens to me."

So when I walked up him, he greeted me with a warm kiss right smack dab in the middle. Honestly, I got so horny that I wanted to unzip his pants and lift up my skirt. But that was just a naughty idea that momentarily zipped through my mind while we were kissing during those everlasting 11 seconds. When he gave me the flowers, I was speechless.

Surprisingly, he looked exactly the same a year ago when I met him in Vegas. His smile was the same, he didn't gain a substantial amount of weight (in other words, he didn't get fat) and those pretty blue eyes were still twinkling like icy blue crystals.

The first few minutes were surreal as we both didn't know what to say. I think I said something like 'Wow, New York, eh?' but my mind turned blank.

"How was your flight?" He said breaking the ice.

"It was fast. How was your flight from Europe?"

"Unlike yours, it was long." He said chuckling.

"I bet. Europe is long ways from here. So how we getting to Manhattan?"

"Let's grab a cab outside." He said while helping me with my luggage.

During the cab ride to Battery Park, we were like little kids continuously giggling, kissing, and realized that we were finally together.

Chapter Forty

Life is Grand

April 21, 2006
Mood: Happy

*W*HEN WE ARRIVED at the Grand Liberty building at Battery Park, I felt like I was in some kind of Wall Street movie. There was a cute Puerto Rican door man who held the door open for us and as we entered the lobby, everything from the Modern Art paintings to the Oriental vases looked so extravagantly put together.

We're staying in suite 2316 situated on the 23rd floor (oh God, I'm so afraid of heights, but I guess I'll have to suck it up).

We have a beautiful view overlooking the New York harbour. The Statue of Liberty and Ground Zero isn't that far away.

While I was admiring the view, Jayden embraced me from behind, "Isn't it great? Can you believe this is our home for the week?"

"Yeah, it's crazy. I feel like it's a dream, the view is breathtaking. Can we afford this?"

"Don't worry, love. This is my producer's condo, he owns it. He stays here when he has business in New York, so we don't owe him anything. I've already stayed here before."

"Really? So this is like your second home."

He chuckled, "I had stayed here before I met you in Vegas."

"But I sure hope that this is your first time hosting a lady companion." I said smiling.

"Of course, you're the first and the last. I told Vlado about us and he gave us his blessing to stay here whenever we want. Except when he comes into town." He laughed.

"I think we're lucky."

"Why?"

"Because we're together again." I said.

"Honestly, I was stressed out when I left Prague. After we spoke on the phone that first time when your friend told you about Duke, I had some doubts that maybe you wouldn't show up."

So he *was* human after all? So relieved to know that he was just as worried as I was, but that's what happens when you have sex with people. You get nervously worried about what they're thinking about you.

"Nah, I wouldn't do that to you. If I wasn't going to show up, I wouldn't be able to forgive myself. I was just shocked by the whole thing. When Neil showed me all your DVD's, I was stunned."

"I know you must've been mad."

"I wasn't mad, I was just confused. I was telling myself that the person I met in Vegas wasn't the person that was in all of these videos."

Complete silence. Here I go again over analyzing everything. He seemed fine when he looked into my eyes, I felt the connection. I learned that sometimes you make connections with people that you can't explain. I do admit that I got turned on, but in my mind, I know that I'm just physically attracted to him and that in no way in hell I'm going to let myself fall in love with him. Get it straight, it's lust not love.

Whatever it was, the time had come, we wanted each other and we spent the afternoon enjoying wild trysts around the suite. First we christened the bed with some foreplay along with some hot oral. It was pretty damn good. His moves, his body, the way he kissed me, it all felt very insatiable like the time we spent in Vegas. When I felt him, I instantly knew that I was hooked. There was something illicit about us hooking up again, but I couldn't control myself, it's like he unleashed my inhibitions. He had that power over me, and, yet, he had this shady past.

*   *   *

But he made up for it, not just in the bedroom, but in the romance department. We just got back from a clandestine dinner at Serendipity on East 60th street and he gave me a Gucci wallet as a surprise. It was a wonderful surprise.

Over dinner, he finally opened up about his life growing up in former Czechoslovakia. He said that he grew up in a poor family in Bratislava. So when his country became independent in the 1990's, he wanted to travel and see the world. One day while he was swimming at Golden Sands beach, he met Vlado, his producer/boss, who befriended him and told him that he was working in the States as an associate producer for a gay porn studio based in Los Angeles called Stetson's Men.

He told Jared that Stetson's Men gave him a budget to produce porn flicks, specifically, with Eastern European men and he thought that Jayden had the right look to become the leading man.

At first, Jayden refused his offer; he thought Vlado was a sick pervert. But they kept in touch and within a year, Vlado convinced him that there were many Americans who were rich and successful shooting gay porn. He told Jayden that if he shot two to three feature movies per year he would be able to buy his own house, buy the Mini-cooper that he was always dreaming about, and he would be able to travel around the world. At that moment, Jayden was impressed with all the perks, especially the travelling benefits. But he told me that the real reason why he did it was for the money because he wanted to go to university and study architecture.

So after a few months of being broke and jobless, Jayden called up Vlado and from there they say the rest is history.

During desert, we engulfed ourselves in a delicious chocolate mousse cake while he reassured me that he retired from acting in 2004. He also came clean and told me about his behind-the-scenes job as a cameraman and editor in Bratislava at Vlado's studio called Bueno Boys. So he's a porn producer for the same company that made him into a star. I couldn't judge him because he's independent. He owns a three-bedroom house near Bratislava Castle and drives two Mini-Coopers. He finished his architectural degree in 2002 and he wants the same things as any normal person wants, marriage and family.

After listening to his story, I appreciated his honesty. He told me that he never wanted to act in porn again and that his behind-the-scenes job was just a temporary gig until he got something better outside the world of porn.

What could I say? I wasn't in the position to judge him; I've also made lousy choices when it came to giving into the temptations of earning fast cash, just look what happened with the show? I was more focused on the dollar signs than the actual job itself, so Jayden felt the same.

So tomorrow is his important photo shoot; he's in bed now and after the conversation we just had, I think it's a good idea to join him and just cuddle. I'm so glad that I came to New York to see him, it's been worth it.

Chapter Forty-One

Photoshoot at Milk Studios

April 21, 2006
Mood: Happy

*W*E JUST WRAPPED up Jayden's photo shoot at Milk Studios on 15th street. All I have to say is WOW. The photographer for the book is well-renowned Timothy Greenfield-Sanders. He's practically shot every celebrity from Halle Berry to politicians like Barack Obama and Hilary Clinton. But today he shot, my love, Jayden for his upcoming book called "30 Porn Star Portraits."

While Jayden was in hair and make-up, Timothy showed me around the studio and told me his vision of his book. He was going to shoot Jayden in the flesh. The book was going to depict each porn star in one nude photograph and another fully-clothed one. That was it. Nothing raunchy or x-rated, only tasteful nude photography, Timothy said.

When Jayden was ready, he came out from the dressing room wearing only a white bathrobe and his street sneakers. After a few light adjustments and test shots, Timothy uttered the golden words, "Alright Jayden let's shoot! Can I ask you to take off the robe?"

And without hesitation Jayden disrobed and stood buck naked in front of me, Timothy, and his four assistants. I sat in the dim corner on some old leather couch just admiring Jayden's confidence (and, of course, his shlong). He was just hanging out, you know, he didn't even seem a tad bit nervous that his manhood was there for the whole world to see.

It was kind of fascinating for me to see this because I had worked in a nude TV show before, never saw it from another point-of-view. So I kind of understood where Jayden was coming from, he was just comfortable with himself with or without clothes on.

There was nothing sleazy or x-rated about it at all. I was enjoying the whole photo shoot. After about an hour, the shoot wrapped up and we went home.

So now we're going out for sushi. After last night's conversation, it's hard for me to walk away from him, because he was honest and kind to me. I haven't felt this good about a person in a very long time.

It's like when we met again in New York, nothing changed since we last saw each other Vegas. It's like the spark was always there, it never died.

After today's shoot, I can say that I've come to terms with Jared's job. But I wonder if he can understand what I'm going through right now being unemployed and having no clear direction in life.

I guess we have another three days to figure things out. Now that the photo shoot is wrapped up, the real fun begins.

*   *   *

That night we had sex in three different places. It started on the couch, then on the kitchen counter, then finally we shagged in the bedroom. The whole time while I was having multiple orgasms it dawned on me that this was the best sex I ever had. What a shit bomb! It's going to be so hard to say goodbye to Jayden. I wish he didn't have to go back to Europe, why can't we just stay here in New York?

Chapter Forty-Two

New York Nights

April 22, 2006
Mood: Excited

*W*E'VE GOT THREE more days here in NYC and I don't want this trip to end. We've been to the Statue of Liberty, Empire State building, and Madame Toussands wax museum.

We're having a blast, but as usual what's bugging me is that in three more days, I have to go back to Toronto to a world of nothing.

I couldn't take it anymore; I had to tell Jayden why I felt so restless, "Baby, can I tell you something that I haven't told anyone before?"

"What?" He said while his blue eyes twinkled.

"I'm afraid that I won't find a good job again."

He embraced me from behind as he admired me in front of our closet full-length mirror, "Look at you . . . you're stunning. You're the most exotic woman in the whole world. You can do anything."

"It doesn't matter how I look, Jayden, are you listening to me?" I turned around and put my arms around him, "I'm done with the show and my TV career is over. Honestly, I don't care about it anymore. I'm thinking about quitting the whole biz forever."

"What do you want to do, instead?"

"I don't know. Maybe I'll write or teach something. That's the thing, I feel so lost. Have you ever asked yourself 'Who am I? Why the fuck am I here in the world?"

"All the time." He said chuckling. "Everyone asks themselves these questions every day."

"So how come I can't find any of the answers?"

"Lezah, look into your heart, and tell me what do you want to do with your life?"

"I don't fucking know!" I shrieked. "That's what I mean. I just see a big question mark. But I know what I *don't* want to do."

"What's that?"

"I don't want to work a 9 to 5 job for some big company. I don't want to model right now. I'm fed up with dead end gigs and feeling uncertain about the next job."

"Hmm, yeah I know your situation is shitty."

"Thanks." I said sarcastically. "That's what I need to hear right now, a reminder of how shitty my situation is."

"I didn't mean it that way. If you're feeling confused about everything, why you don't just come back with me to Europe and hang out for a while?"

Those words were like magic to my ears. Suddenly, I heard the angels chanting "Alleluia! Alleluia!" and I had a vision of us lying together on a deserted beach while sipping on margaritas and making love.

"Really, you want me to come with you to Europe?" I said snapping out of my brief haze.

"Yes, of course. I don't want to leave you out here."

"You understand that I have no job in Toronto and maybe some time in Europe might give me some insight. I promise I'll be good to you." I said flirtatiously.

"You better be good. I want breakfast every morning and a massage every day when I come home from work." He jokingly demanded.

"Anything you want, I can do it all from random blow jobs to cooking you delicious Filipino dishes." I lied about the cooking, so mental note: must find some online recipes and also ring Mom for her amazing cooking tips on chicken Adobo.

"Ah, just as long as you don't burn anything, I'll be happy. Well what about the writing thing?"

"I do want to become a writer, but you need time to become a good writer."

"But isn't that what you have now? All the free time in the world to do what you want?"

He was right. That *was* true. After all this time of dicking around, maybe it was time to focus on writing. I could write about my experience in the biz and it'll destroy every young hopeful model's dream about becoming a huge star. Talk about being cynical.

"Come here." He said comforting me with a soft kiss on the lips, "Now don't worry about what will happen to you. Believe in destiny and enjoy the moment. I don't want you to get wrinkles from all the unnecessary worrying. You're with me now and that's all that matters." He said with reassuring eyes.

God, you have no idea how long I waited to hear those words uttered from his mouth. Finally, I could let my hair down and breathe.

After this day forward, I denounce myself from the biz and dedicate my life to travelling the world. But most of all, I'm going to Europe to find myself and, hopefully, find love with Jayden.

*   *   *

It's our last night here in NYC and Jayden has this wild idea to go to a swinger's club. Apparently, he got invited from one of Timothy's assistants to come to The Big Swing at the Meatpacking District.

I'm gung ho for it, I've never been to anything so wild and underground. The most fascinating night club I've been to was when fetish night was hosted at the Guvernment in Toronto a few years ago. But then again, it wasn't that shocking. I saw a man walking on all fours strapped in a dog collar being walked by some Elvira looking chick. She also held a flogger and from time to time when she whipped his ass, a loud bam echoed amongst the crowd.

Other than that, the show was lame and I saw over a million women wearing the same black latex dress that night. After seeing the same dress over and over that night, I was convinced that I was *never* going to have that dress hanging in my closet any time soon.

So here we are in New York and I am hoping that my experience at The Big Swing will be different. We're both decked out in black and he wants us wear these masks that I remember seeing in the sex scenes of "Eyes Wide Shut." It sounds to me like we're going to have a very interesting night. "We're going in as voyeurs." He told me today. So the date is set, I'm game but we've got to catch our flight tomorrow morning at 8 am. Oh God, I hope I don't wake up in some other couple's bed.

Chapter Forty-Three

The End is the Beginning

April 23, 2006
Mood: Excited

*I*T'S 7 O'CLOCK in the morning and we're already at La Guardia. We practically came home in our party clothes and left the apartment in a hurry to get here. The Manhattan beat is so fast that I can't keep up.

Well, what can I say about last night? It was strangely erotic and a little scary with all the S&M victims and masters.

I felt utterly out of place at the swinger's party. I kept telling myself to stop being a prude and try to join in on the fun. But it wasn't filled with so many couples having sex with other couples. That's probably true in Amsterdam, but last night, I just saw a lot of S&M acts being performed on people.

There was this bald Asian lady, she reminded me of a Harley Davidson monk (If that even exists out there). As she strolled around in the night club dressed in a spiked collar and all-leather outfit, she approached different kinds of women with a rider's crop and started parlaying the crop on the woman's arm—trying to entice her.

One blond, who was obviously some wannabe New York starlet, started kissing the Asian woman in front of everyone. The Asian woman lured her to a corner of the club and a crowd formed immediately as Mistress Mimi began tying up the blond socialite with leather straps on some couch.

Mistress Mimi then transformed into some seasoned performer and announced to all of us, "Now you shall see my slave feel the utmost pleasure through extreme pain."

I was getting excited and Jayden held me close as we witnessed Mistress Mimi tightening the leather straps on the blond's body. Her face became red as the dominatrix wrapped another leather strap across her victim's mouth. Her hands were tied from the back and when Mistress Mimi positioned the blond to kneel on all fours she began torturing her victim with different kinds of whips. She whipped her so hard that we saw how red her ass got after several lashes. Ouch, I bet that girl's ass is stinging today.

After the whipping session, Mistress Mimi took out some torture devices and after rubbing her victim's nipples, she clamped them with some nipple clamps. Ouch again! I felt that when the blond squirmed, but with the leather constraint in her mouth, I saw the sides of her mouth were salivating. She was enjoying the BDSM slave humiliation.

After the nipple clamp scene, the novelty had worn off and Jayden took me to a part of the club where some couples were dressed up in cartoon character costumes. It was so messed up. Just a minute ago we went from being in some kind of warped world of Misstress Mimi to a live cartoon show with bright studio lights on a plush white couch.

There was a couple dressed up in life-sized Popeye and Olive costumes. We couldn't see their faces, their real identities hidden inside the confines of their costumes. Very funny.

I remember going to Disney World when I was a teenager and running up to Mickey and Minnie Mouse with a great big hug. That was the last time I saw life sized cartoon characters in action.

So when Popeye and Olive started making out on the plush couch, a crowd formed around them, and after a dry humping display of affection, Popeye just pulled out his dick from the costume and began shagging Olive underneath her dress. Bizarre! It was so weird because it felt like I was watching a live cartoon porno with one of my favourite cartoon heroes—Popeye! Well, to say the least, it was freaky. I mean we all know that Mickey and Minnie and Miss Piggy and Kermit the Frog are couples. But to see Popeye's head bobbing back and forth smoking on that pipe while he bangs his sweet old Olive on a staged bed, well, let's just say that I won't ever look at a cartoon the same way again.

Throughout the whole night we had our masquerade masks on and when I looked at Jayden's reaction when we watched all these people give into their fetishes, he seemed bored as if he had already been there and done that.

I keep forgetting that he's lived this porn star lifestyle, so going to these sex parties was no treat for him, probably just part of the game.

But I enjoyed seeing people's reaction when fulfilling their sexual fantasies. At times, it made me wonder what were my deepest and darkest fantasies? I guess castle sex would be it. I've always wanted to join the mile high club. Something sci-fi would do it for me like having sex in outer space with an alien.

This early in the morning, it's hard to tell what my sexual fantasies are. But I do know that some of them are going to be fulfilled because this is it, I'm going to Europe! Nobody knows back home that I'm going with him. It's not like they would care anyways, they know I can take care of myself. With no job, no prospects, and no direction in where I want to go, maybe this swinger's show was all I needed. I needed to see that people do let go of their inhibitions. Maybe that's why I'm so fucked up because I can't set myself free. I can't let go. So wound up and worried about what other people say.

That's why Jayden is heaven sent. I know I'm crazy staying with him, but for once in my life, I actually *like* him. I know other women who wouldn't fathom dating a former gay porn star; I know I'm taking an enormous risk getting involved with someone like him. But it's done, I'm already into deep.

We just got our boarding call flight 35 to Prague, Czech Republic. So this is it. I'm leaving New York and North America all together to join this man. I don't know if I'm crazy or just in love. Or just totally impulsive with my already pathetic life. I'm saying goodbye to biz and saying hello to Europe with a new man. Who knows, maybe in Europe I'll do something completely different with my life. Jayden says that he'll be with me every step of the way. Something tells me that I should trust him. But only time will tell. See you on the other side of the world.

To Be Continued